I0450939

Unsuited

Tressie Lockwood

Amira Press

Unsuited
Tressie Lockwood

Publisher:
Amira Press
North Carolina, USA
www.amirapress.com

Unsuited

Chapter One

"Nyah, your boy's here," her friend Tracy called out to her.

Nyah rolled her eyes and finished wiping oil from her fingers. She didn't need Tracy to point out the car that just pulled up. She could see it for herself, and who could miss it? He drove a 1969 Shelby GT500 with a rebuilt engine and dual pistons. The first time she saw it, she loved it. That baby could go from zero to sixty in 3.5 seconds. But more than the sweet ride was the man who owned it. The mechanical body was in pristine condition, just like the hard, masculine body that was unfolding from it now.

Ethan Daniels was sexy as hell. He wore tailored suits—at least that's how she viewed them. They weren't cheap. That's for sure. The material snuggled against his solid form, across his shoulders and big chest. And he smelled good. When she stood near him, it was all she could do not to throw herself into his arms just to breathe the man in.

By now, Tracy knew Ethan was like a fix for her. Every few months he came in for a checkup. Over the last year and a half, she'd never missed his visits, but if she had, she'd have wept like a little girl.

The bell to the office dinged as he came in, and it was her turn at the counter. A dull pain started up in her belly, and her hands were clammy. Nyah watched him stroll toward her and kept her eyes trained on his face. Eyes aqua like the waters she saw in the Bahamas the one time she visited, a strong clean-shaven jaw line, and lips she wanted to explore with kisses like nobody's business. He drew close to the counter, and even being on the opposite side she had to look up. Six four or five?

"Hello, Nyah. How are you?" he asked in deep, panty-wetting tones.

He knew her name. Of course it was written on her jumper, but since she was staring into his eyes, she knew he hadn't looked down. He remembered from his previous visits. She almost responded with "Hi, Ethan" but caught herself. She needed to maintain her professionalism or get in trouble with her stickler of a boss. "Hello, Mr. Daniels. I'm fine, thanks. I hope your day is going great so far."

Grr, I sound like I have a stick up my butt. But he smiled as if she'd said something clever. Ethan didn't flirt, but he had a way of making her feel like she was something special. The feeling was probably all in her head, but a woman had to enjoy it where she could sometimes.

"It's pulling to the right a bit. Can you take a look at it?" he asked. The warmth in his gaze drew her in.

"Anything for you," she murmured, but at his startled expression, she cleared her throat and turned to the computer screen to pull up his account. "I mean, of course. Sounds like you might need an alignment, or it could be the brakes. Let me check on the last time you had them looked at."

Her fingers flew over the keys typing in his phone number. She was pathetic to know it. Not that dealing with a few regulars didn't ingrain their info into her head, but most of those others were by address or name. To memorize Ethan's cell number was too lame. The man probably didn't know she was a woman outside of general terms like the fact that her voice was high and her name had a feminine ring to it. The work clothes all the mechanics wore was a bland blue with no style, and her boss didn't allow any jewelry while on the job. If she at least had a big butt and big boobs, that might stand out, but she didn't. Nyah was built like her mother with a slender figure, and not until she met Ethan did she care one way or another. Now it felt like a curse.

She printed off the work order for him to sign and slipped it across the counter. When he reached out to straighten the paper, his fingers brushed hers. Nyah's heart raced, and she chewed her bottom lip. Pure desire for him brought her body to life, and she jerked back, keeping her eyes on the sheet.

"Sorry about that," he whispered.

She looked up at him trying to read his expression, but it was impossible. Ethan had always been kind, but he never gave any indication that he was attracted to her. Tracy pushed her to make the first move by inviting him to dinner, but she knew if he was offended or turned off, he could report her to her boss, and she could get fired. That was a big risk. Something told her a man like Ethan wouldn't be so unkind even if he wasn't interested, but she was still scared. She was blue collar to his white, and aside from that he was a white man. Who knew if he'd ever considered dating a black woman?

While she watched him sign wishing she wasn't so chicken to open up her mouth, the bell over the door dinged again. She glanced past Ethan to see a tall, beautiful woman stepping inside. She raised a hand to flick long chestnut hair back over her shoulder and removed her dark sunglasses. She scanned the place and then settled on Ethan. If there were flashing cameras and a fan to blow her hair as she walked, she wouldn't have been out of place, Nyah thought. The woman was style and class. She wore high heels with cute little pink polished toes peeking out the front. Her skirt suit was just as much quality by the look of it as Ethan's was. They were a matched set and looked like a couple. All the sunshine of Nyah's morning just faded away.

"Hey, Ethan," the woman said when she stopped beside him. "Did you call Luke to pick us up?" Of course she just had to lay a hand on Ethan's arm in that possessive way. *Okay, we all know he's yours.* Nyah wanted to add a silent "bitch" to the end of that thought, but refrained. He didn't belong to her, and she'd not even tried to get his attention, so she was out of luck.

Irritated, Nyah thanked Ethan in a clipped tone and snatched up the work order to take it to the back. She made it to the side door before she remembered she hadn't taken his keys. Mouthing a curse, she turned back to find him facing her holding them out. One eyebrow rose, and he wore a smirk, but the light in his eyes was still friendly.

As she took them, thanking him and avoiding impact with his fingers, he murmured, "Cheer up. You have the rest of the day to get through."

For some reason, she laughed. "I don't know if that's encouragement or you're telling me it's all downhill from here."

He winked. "Take your pick."

That was a first. A shiver of delight zinged over her, raising goose bumps. The tall and beautiful woman looked from him to Nyah and back then frowned. She leaned in closer to him and took his arm again. "So tonight, you want Chinese or Italian?"

His girlfriend, Nyah concluded. She froze, then balled the keys in a tight fist, and spun away. When would she get it through her head? A man like him was not looking in her direction.

When Nyah pushed through the side door to head to the back, Tracy accosted her, dragging her out of direct view of the customer waiting area. "So? Did you do it? Did you ask him out?"

Nyah frowned. "Girl, you don't know me very well, do you? No, I didn't. But I'm glad I didn't because he has a girlfriend."

Tracy smacked her forehead and closed her eyes as if in denial. Now who was being dramatic. "No!"

"Yep." She put the work order on the desk beside a second computer and noted that Mustafa was just bringing in the GT500. More annoyance ate at her. "Just look at the leggy piece hanging from his arm out there. I didn't have a chance anyway."

Tracy stomped over to her and pulled her closer to the window that allowed them to view the customers and vice versa. "If you stop feeling like you're not his type. Take a look. When she walked up on him and grabbed his arm, he didn't even look her way. And see? He's concentrating on his phone, not her. I see a one way attraction there, and it's all on her side."

Nyah sighed. "That's because you're a romantic. I'm practical. What I see is a man who's had that, and he's not interested in more, but she's fallen in love with him, and she can't let go."

Tracy laughed, planting her hands on her hips. "We're bad, aren't we? I say you're wrong, but you keep thinking that, and you're going to lose out. Just ask yourself one thing. Why would you be this attracted, this long to a man who'd keep a woman stringing along? That's not you, and he would have shown his true colors months ago."

Nyah wasn't sure if Tracy was right or not. The fact was she didn't see Ethan all that often, and it was always in a professional capacity. She didn't have the opportunity to find out if he was a good guy or a bad one. Either way, she had work to do, and she pushed Mr. Ethan Daniels out of mind until she had to report back on his car.

Chapter Two

Nyah hadn't been able to get how cute that woman's toes looked out of her head. Now she sat on her couch with the big screen TV blaring an episode of *Grey's Anatomy* and at the same time trying to polish her toes bright red. Her big toe was smeared. The second one looked much darker than the first, and in her frustration, she'd in essence colored outside of the lines with the rest. "So not cute," she muttered just as her cell phone rang.

She picked up seeing that it was Tracy calling. Her friend didn't give her the chance to say hello. "We're going out. What are you wearing?"

Nyah laughed. "Old, ratty gym shorts and a tank top. Plus I tried painting my toenails for the first time since I was six, and they look a fright."

"Girl, are you crazy?" Tracy's frown was clear in her tone. "If you wanted to come over to the feminine side like I've been harassing you to do for the last five years, you should have said something! We can go get our fingernails and toes done at my nail place."

"See, now you've gone too far," Nyah muttered. She closed the cap on the polish, having come to the conclusion that she was hopeless at this stuff. At least she'd bought remover and cotton balls at the store, or she'd be in big trouble. During the warmer months, she normally wore sandals when not at work, but her nails were now stained reddish pink for the time being. If they were going out, she'd have to wear sneakers or something. "Where do you want to go? A movie? I thought we decided nothing good was playing right now."

Tracy's voice took on a mischievous tone. "Just somewhere. A bar. Come with me, please. I need a drink after dealing with Jeff the Wonder Boss all week. And for once, we're both off at the same time on the weekend. It's mandatory that we take advantage of it."

Tracy always called their boss Jeff the Wonder Boss because of his overly enthusiastic attitude about everything they did and how each task had to be done a precise way. He was part of the reason she hadn't asked Ethan out at work. Jeff would have her butt in the unemployment line scared he was going to be sued for sexual harassment.

"Okay, since you put it that way, I'll come. I have nothing better to do anyway."

"Thanks a lot, Nyah. You make me feel so special."

Nyah chuckled. Tracy's feelings were never easily hurt. She was one of the most confident people Nyah knew, and if she hadn't forbidden her friend from approaching Ethan on her behalf, Tracy would already have blurted out how she felt about him.

"I'll be there in an hour. Try to girlie it up a bit, K?" She hung up before Nyah could tell her she didn't "girlie" anything up—*ever*. She sighed and put her phone down. No sense arguing. She'd be herself, and Tracy would do the same. They accepted each other on the whole and had been friends forever, so she wasn't worried about it. Nyah stood to go to her room to find something decent. She already knew the kinds of clothes she loved to wear and was pretty sure nothing would meet with Tracy's approval.

* * * *

Nyah walked into the bar alongside Tracy. The place was on the small side but already packed wall to wall. They found a table near the back and sat down. Tracy took her wallet from her purse and slid the purse across the table. "I'm going to go get us something to drink. What do you want?"

"Irish car bomb and a Hawaiian screw." Nyah handed her the money, and she watched her friend squeeze through the crowd. For some reason, instead of going straight to the bar, Tracy circled it while looking around. Nyah rolled her eyes. If that girl had set up some kind of blind date for her, she was going to wring her neck.

But Tracy came back alone with the drinks. She did display an excited grin, which made Nyah suspicious. She didn't have long to wonder as Tracy leaned across the table toward her. "Take a look over my shoulder, like diagonally away from you."

Nyah frowned. She searched the area pointed out and froze. There was Ethan, just as sexy as she remembered him. And like she would have guessed he was still in a collared shirt and slacks. The only thing missing was the tie and the jacket, but he looked good. His hair was a little less ordered, with a tussled look like he'd rolled out of bed moments ago. Probably did, she guessed, with the bevy of beautiful women around him. In fairness, it did look like he was also partying with a few male friends. Of course the brunette from a few days ago was in the group.

"So he's here. Whatever." She downed her shot and then sipped her Hawaiian screw. Tracy looked guilty. "Please tell me this is just a coincidence."

Tracy shrugged. "I found out where he likes to hang out."

"How?"

"Don't question the sources or they will not be there when you need them."

Nyah laughed. "Okay, Flat Foot. Anyway, it makes no difference. You said that woman wasn't anything special. So what's she doing here?"

"It's Friday night. Everybody unwinds after they get off. I bet she tagged along when somebody mentioned they were coming here. Since it wasn't a date, he could hardly say no."

"You're determined to excuse him." Nyah shook her head and then began rocking to the loud music. "Listen, if you find him that appealing, you go talk to him. I'm going to order some onion rings. I don't think I ate enough dinner, and I'm not going to be under this table because of it, with a hangover tomorrow."

Nyah leaned on the bar with both elbows and went up to her tiptoes. She signaled to the bartender and placed her order. By the time she turned around to survey the scene, she was face-to-face with Ethan. Her heart stuttered in her chest. He smiled.

"Hello."

"Hey," she responded. His gaze slipped down from her face to her shirt, and she fidgeted with discomfort. She looked nothing like those women he was with. Every one of them wore short skirts with as much thigh as possible exposed. Their silk blouses were unbuttoned practically to their navels, and they showed off so much boob, there couldn't be much left everyone in the room hadn't seen already with a glance.

"Nice shirt," he said of her Notre Dame T-shirt. Tracy had bought it for her and ended up purchasing it too small, which had made Nyah wonder what her friend thought of her size—childlike probably. The material was skin tight, and the most she could say of it was that it showed up the fact that she hadn't worn a bra. She'd coupled the shirt with jeans.

Nyah smirked up at Ethan. "Thanks. You too."

He moved alongside her, standing close. His male scent assaulted her nose. She couldn't pinpoint the cologne, but it was something expensive and oh so nice. He leaned down close to her ear so he wouldn't have to shout over the music. "Wanna dance?"

"People don't really dance here. Just stand around and drink and talk."

He pointed out a few exceptions to her statement. "They are."

"And they're drunk as hell."

They both laughed.

Nyah spun around to accept her onion rings and began eating them after offering him some. He declined. She chewed the delicious, greasy snack and swallowed before licking a bit of ketchup off her finger. Ethan seemed intrigued by the movement. "Anyway, I'm sure your girlfriend wouldn't like us dancing together."

Only after she said it she wished she hadn't. He must realize she was fishing to know for sure, which in turn revealed that she was interested. She stuffed another ring into her mouth. Eating onions wasn't the best idea when picking up a man, but what the hell. She'd never done what women usually did to get them anyway. If a man was interested, he was. If he wasn't, she moved on. Most of the time, she was happy with who she was, and that was not a lady.

"Girlfriend?" Ethan said. He reached past her hand to snag an onion ring and popped it into his mouth. She was mesmerized with his sexy lips as he chewed. A bit of ketchup lay in the center of his bottom one, and she longed to lick it off. He did the deed, making her want a lot more as she followed the movements of his tongue.

Nyah snapped out of her trance and gave a quick point over to the area he'd come from. "The tall, leggy one with the long hair. She was at the shop with you, and she mentioned having dinner with you. *Okay, seriously, Nyah, shut the hell up. He doesn't need to know you remember every detail.*

His slow grin said he already figured out she was interested. He moved closer with his elbow on the bar. Less than half a dozen inches separated them. "She's not my girlfriend. She's a coworker, and her mention of food had to do with a company meeting we were attending that night. There were at least ten others present."

Nyah lowered her eyes and bit her bottom lip. She fiddled with the rings although she didn't attempt to eat anymore. "You seem pretty determined to clear up that little misunderstanding. But she wants you. That's plain for anybody to see."

"Nothing's ever happened between us, and it never will. I've known Mandy for years, but I think of her as a friend only." He leaned so close this time, that his lips almost touched hers. Now she wished she had a Tic Tac or a piece of gum, but he didn't appear put off in the least. "So, are you convinced, or should I kiss you to prove I'm not taken?"

Her eyes widened. She stared up at him, a deer caught in the headlights of his charm. Of course she wanted a kiss. No, not now. She almost groaned in frustration. "That won't be necessary. I believe you."

He took her hand and pulled her away from the bar. She considered resisting but didn't have the ability to.

Drifting into his arms was heaven on earth, and the solid feel of his chest muscles under her palms sent quakes all over her body. Nyah kept her head down as he moved her closer into his embrace and began to sway side to side. She rocked with him to the soothing rhythm of the music. Somewhere in the back of her lust haze, she registered that she didn't have to correct him. He knew where the beat was.

All eyes in the room must be on them, especially his group and Tracy. But his hand at her lower back began teasing the sensitive area in a way she'd never felt before. Desire crept over her, making it impossible to think rationally. Her body had come alive. Her nipples tingled and had hardened to the point that each time his chest brushed them, jolts of pleasure zinged down between her legs. She had no doubt that her panties were good and ruined. And at that moment, if he asked her to go home with him, she would.

Snap out of it, Nyah. Don't even think like that.

"What are you thinking?" he asked as if he was already privy to her thoughts.

"Nothing."

He raised her chin. She was swept away in the depths of his eyes. She loved white men and had dated one once. He'd turned out to be a jerk, but it didn't change how attractive she found them. Smooth tanned skin, colorful eyes, silky hair. She knew those were superficial reasons, but she'd dated duds of a few different races and couldn't say one race was better or worse.

"I see it in your eyes," he said watching her.

"You see what?"

He smirked. "You want me."

She wrinkled her nose. "So you think you're all that, huh?" His attitude didn't annoy her. Hell, the man was hot. No use denying it, and he hadn't said what he did in a superior way. More like stating the obvious.

"I'm just calling it like I see it, but I'm not afraid to admit I want you too." His gaze dropped to her breasts. "You should know that I've been with black women before."

"Oh is that right?"

"Yes, that's right." He lowered his hand to the curve of her ass. "It wouldn't be culture shock."

Nyah clenched her jaw. She raised her hands from his chest to his shoulders and then hugged him. He was so much taller than she was that the top of her head reached just past his chin. What an amazing turn-on. His cock pressed into her belly, already hard. The temptation to take this to where they both wanted it to go was strong, but one-night stands didn't do it for her. Yet somehow she knew he didn't want to date either. He'd said he'd been with black women, not that he'd dated them. Maybe he hadn't ever dated. He might be the kind of man who chose a lover and stuck with her for as long as his interest held, and then he was gone.

With effort, she broke their eye contact and turned her head to rest on his chest. "So what are you saying?"

She didn't know if he'd heard her over the noise of

the bar since he took a long time answering, but she didn't want to push either. This could be just a dance, a tease. After all, they weren't on the same professional level. While classes didn't exist on the surface anymore, there was that unspoken thing where people of like backgrounds tended to get together. None of that mattered for a quick fuck.

"Come outside with me," he said and took her hand to pull her behind him. They weaved through the crowd toward the exit. Nyah made eye contact with Tracy and raised her shoulders at the question in her friend's gaze.

When they were outside, Nyah drew in a steadying breath. The air wasn't exactly cool, but it did feel a little less stuffy than the atmosphere of the bar. She followed Ethan along the side of the building and expected him to turn at any second to explain what he wanted from her. Instead he spun and took her in his arms. All the air she'd just breathed in whooshed from her lungs at the impact of his chest. The man didn't even know his own strength. Not that she was complaining or anything.

She tilted her head back a little to meet his gaze. And even if she was a green girl who didn't know what a man's expressions meant, she would have comprehended the open lust in his eyes.

"You have a very bad habit, little miss mechanic."

Her eyebrows went up. "What do you mean?"

His gaze lowered to her lips, and pings of awareness rocketed all over her body. Talk about trying to survive. The man sucked away all of the available air just looking at her. *So out of my league.*

"Every time you get nervous or you're working out an issue, you chew that cute little bottom lip there, and it drives me nuts," he accused. "Do you know how many hard-ons I've had to battle when I come into your shop?"

"Um?" She was at a loss for words. What did she say to that? *Thanks?* Trying to play it cool, she told him, "I apologize. I didn't mean to torment you, but a woman can't help the effect she has on the men around her."

His slow grin made her think the cause and effect principle went both ways. "Is that right?"

She gave a small *que sara sara* shrug. "Pretty much."

"In that case, you cannot blame a man when he does this…" Nyah didn't have a chance to say a word. He slanted his mouth over hers and proceeded to devour her lips. Nyah gave herself up to it, giving as much as she got. Because he was so much taller, she stretched up onto her toes and pressed in closer to his body. Her lips parted in invitation to his tongue. And once he took advantage of it, she pushed hers into his mouth as well.

Hungry lust had her trembling, wanting so much more than this. She tangled her fingers in his hair and luxuriated in its silky smoothness. Not too long or too short, it curled around her fingers, and she held on even as he began running his hot mouth down her neck, to tease the pulse at her throat. Nyah didn't have a doubt in her mind that with this man sex would be explosive. She'd find herself teetering on sanity and pleading for him to take her regularly. But where would that leave her heart?

At last he raised his head and stepped back a little. His

hands never left her hips, and his blue eyes assessed the damage he'd done—to her lips and to her psyche, from the looks of it. The man was probably practiced at seducing women.

"So my place or yours?" he offered.

The question was a cold bucket of water in her face. Nyah moved out of his hold and put all of her weight into one leg, a hand at her hip. "You're assuming I'm going to jump into bed with you right off the bat?"

He couldn't look more surprised. "Come on, honey, you felt what happened just now. The attraction is there in spades, and we're both adults—"

"So because we're both adults, I should be fine fucking you without even a date?" It wasn't like she hadn't done it before. Hell, she'd once jumped into bed with a man whose name she couldn't remember a minute after he told her. But she had been so turned on, she didn't care, and it had been a long time. For a while, she'd hop every time he called, just booty calls late at night, on the weekend. Her place, his, it didn't matter. And it wasn't like that kind of thing would never happen again if she was horny enough. But the fact was no woman chose that. She wanted someone special in her life. She wanted to be able to say she had a boyfriend for a change. Ethan wasn't offering that kind of relationship and might never want it with her. She did have a choice though—take what he offered. At least she could work out the sexual attraction she had for him and know that she'd tapped him once or twice.

"I didn't mean to offend you." He reached for her, but

she turned away and walked toward the bar entrance. He caught her hand before she reached it. "Go out with me. To dinner."

She longed to tell him no he'd already ruined it, but she wanted to go. They would have nothing to talk about. The conversation would be awkward, and he'd come on to her all night or expect that she was putting out at the end of the date. She peered at him over her shoulder, doubtful. He was so beautiful though. Why couldn't she be like him, just take it, sure that there would be no emotional attachments, and have fun?

"Okay, Boardwalk Billy's, and you don't wear a collared shirt. You wear a T-shirt and jeans, and you're buying." She tried suppressing her smile, but it curved her lips up on one side. Ethan matched it with one of his own that had her heart beating faster. Yeah, this was so not a good idea.

"Done," he agreed. He tugged his phone from his pocket and punched a few buttons. When he looked up, those eyes that got her panties wet locked on her. "Your number?"

Nyah provided the information and pretended to wait for his. She already knew his cell from work, but she hadn't programmed it into her phone. That would be stalking. Of course if she was going to stalk any man, Ethan's fine ass was the one to go with.

She left him standing there because she couldn't take another minute in his presence without telling him she'd changed her mind. They could skip dinner and get right to dessert. No way was she handing herself over like that. If she wasn't good enough for dinner, then she wasn't good enough to sleep with either.

Now to get through Miss Tracy's gloating.

Chapter Three

"Girl, please, you know daggone well he's never heard of Boardwalk Billy's," Tracey commented while they skimmed the clothes at It's Fashion.

Nyah sucked her teeth. "He might have." Then she started laughing. "I know right? He probably goes to those ritzier restaurants, places where they have a dress code. But that's exactly why I made sure he would wear a T-shirt and jeans. No dressing up. I like to be casual, and if I'm too casual for him, then I'm not the woman he should be sniffing around."

"See that's why you ain't got no man, Nyah. You're too hard on them."

Nyah wrinkled her nose and rolled her eyes at her friend. They joked, but she knew she wasn't like that. Well not every time. She'd been played by some losers and caught some in the middle of their games. She'd had her heart broken, but she liked to think she didn't carry around a lot of baggage like mistreating a guy because of what the old one did. The fact was, finding the right man was hard as hell no matter what the woman looked like. All of it was a numbers game, and she had to stay in it to ever hope to find someone special.

Nyah held up a slinky knit tank. The front had rhinestones that made up the Y neckline, and the material was bunched around the breasts, which she hoped would make hers look a bit bigger. She liked the back most of all because of the crisscrossed straps and that her shoulders would be out. "What do you think of this?" she asked Tracy.

"I think you wrong for making him wear a tee while you get to be all classy."

"Please, this is just a simple tank. I'm putting it with jeans." She chewed her lip while examining the top. "Although I did pick up that polka dot mini the other day. I don't know. Showing off my stick legs…"

Tracy swiped the blouse from her hand and waved it in the air toward the associate. "She wants to try this on please." She turned back to Nyah. "You are not going to wear that skirt. I had to almost blackmail you to get it. I know it's going to sit in your closet until the moths eat it like every other dress you own."

"I don't own any dresses."

Tracy smirked. "I rest my case."

They made a few purchases, Nyah choosing jewelry to match the blouse. Usually she didn't bother much with it because she couldn't wear it at work, and when she was off, she just forgot. Back at her car, she glanced at her fingernails. No matter how she scrubbed them, they just didn't look as pristine as most women's. There was always a spot of grease she missed somewhere. And the nails themselves would make a nail technician cry out in horror.

She unlocked the doors on her car and hopped in with Tracy slipping into the passenger side. Her cell phone rang, and Nyah dumped her bags into the back seat before pulling out her phone. She frowned at the display. What the heck did her boss want?

Nyah answered. "Hello, Jeff. What's up?" She raised her eyebrows in Tracy's direction, and her friend frowned.

"Hi, Nyah, I wanted to talk to you about something." His tone was still that over the top enthusiastic way he had, but she detected a note of caution too. Like he was dealing with a wild animal that could attack at any time. Nyah had never given him any reason to treat her that way, so she was really beginning to worry.

"What about?"

"I understand you're seeing one of our clients," he began.

Calm left, but Nyah held it together. "And?"

He hesitated. "And you understand how important our clients are—especially the ones with custom-made vehicles. We're not the only service center in this big city, so we want to go the extra mile with them, give them special treatment."

"I thought I *was* giving him special treatment." She couldn't resist, visualizing his flaming red face. Jeff, as off the wall as he was, would not miss the innuendo. "I'm not sure how who I see and who I don't has anything to do with you."

By that time, Tracy was signaling to her to explain, and when Nyah waved her off, she leaned in close to try to pick up Jeff's side of the conversation.

His agitation was plain in his voice when he spoke again. "It has everything to do with me when you met this man at my company, and maybe even accessed private information to contact him."

"Whoa, hold up," she growled. "You need to stop jumping to conclusions about what I did and didn't do. For all you know I could have met him before he ever became a client, and I could have told him about your company. But aside from all that, I want to know who the hell told you I was seeing him in the first place."

"It was an anonymous tip."

"Anonymous tip, my ass," she belted back. Tracy laid a hand on her arm as a signal for her to calm down. Nyah made an effort, but it didn't work. "I have a right to know who is talking behind my back, obviously trying to jeopardize my livelihood."

"Yes, your livelihood," Jeff pointed out. For the first time, the enthusiasm drifted away and he spoke like a normal person. "You should be thinking about your job instead of worrying over who told me about Ethan Daniels."

"You're threatening to fire me based on my sex life?" she shouted across the line. "You cannot be serious!"

"No one said anything about firing." She wasn't sure if he was trying to soothe her anger or keep control of the conversation.

"I'm one of the best mechanics you have. Hell, half the guys there have their lame-ass hootchies showing up all times of the day, and you don't say anything to them." Her boss made no comment to this, and she went on. "No, this is about you potentially losing money if he gets mad at me and never wants to come to the shop again. That's what it is, right? And he's got friends that he might influence?"

"I'm glad we understand each other."

She gritted her teeth. "I don't think we do. I—"

"Good-bye, Nyah. I hope you have a great weekend, and I'll see you bright and early on Monday morning." He hung up.

Nyah stared at the phone in disbelief. Her hands shook. Not from fear or sadness, but from rage. "Oh no he fucking didn't," she pushed between gritted teeth. "Tracy, I'm going to have to take you home instead of us going to my place. I have to swing by the job and have a little talk with Jeff."

"Uh-uhn, girl, you not dropping me off. I'm going with you. If you punch him in the throat, I want to be there to see it."

Nyah laughed. "Fine. And crazy, I'm not going to punch him, but I am planning to give him something real to fire me for. Nobody's going to tell me who to see and who not to. Who the hell does he think he is anyway?"

Tracy's excitement bubbled up so much she practically

bounced in her seat. Nyah shook her head, turned over the car engine, and took off. She couldn't get to her job fast enough. Didn't he know that she'd turned down offers to come work at other shops? Please, she was good at what she did, and his threats weren't going to fly. In fact, she guessed that's why he hung up so fast, to keep the upper hand. Whatever! She was about to rip it off and beat him with it.

When she screeched into the parking lot, the heads of her coworkers popped up from the various bays where they worked on cars. A couple of them smiled and waved. Tracy shouted greetings. Nyah gave a curt nod and headed through to the manager's office.

"Oh, he's not in there, Nyah," one of the guys called out. He pointed a thumb in the direction of the employee bathroom. "Been in there a bit."

Nyah stomped over to the bathroom and banged on the door. "Jeff, I need to talk to you!" If all eyes weren't on her already, they were now, even the clients. She didn't care. "Jeff!"

"Just a minute," he yelled back. She heard the nervousness in his tone and considered pressing it home by rattling the handle but held off. Soon enough she would give him a piece of her mind. She took a few steps back from the door and crossed her arms over her chest while tapping her foot. The toilet flushed, and she heard the faucet turn on. After a few minutes, Jeff emerged, his cheeks crimson.

Nyah started in. "I don't know who you think you're

dealing with threatening me, but—"

"Let's take this in my office," he suggested.

"Why, so no one can hear how you tried to run my personal life and decide who I date, and if I don't listen to you I lose my job? Which one of the men here have you done that to? Which one? Because I know any one of those guys would have belted you in the mouth."

"Nyah," Jeff groaned. His skin color had grown mottled. "My office, *please*."

She sucked her teeth. "Fine."

They headed into his office, and he shut the door on the curious stares all around. Before Nyah lost sight of everyone, she caught Tracy's gleaming smile, and her friend threw a thumbs-up sign at her. Nyah wasn't sure what she mouthed, but she could guess it was something like "chew him up and spit him out." Tracy was crazy like that.

"Have a seat," he offered and took his own chair.

"No thanks." She wasn't going to act like he was the big powerful boss, and she was the lowly employee who was at his mercy. "I guess you don't know how many offers I turned down to work here. Even after I hired on. I'm damn good even if I am a woman. I've proven myself tons of times, *and* I have loyal clients that will walk with me if I ever decide to leave this shop."

Jeff's mouth dropped open.

"Yeah, that's right." She slammed her hands down on his desk. "I'm always respectful of you. I don't get into all the backbiting and talking behind your back. That's not my style. But I'll be damned if you think you can manipulate me. So I want to know who the hell told you I was going out with Ethan Daniels."

"I don't think that has anything—"

"Who?" she growled.

He hesitated, and his agitated gaze dropped from her face to his desktop while he shuffled papers around. When the fact that she bore down over him made the man jumpy, he surged to his feet, shoved his hands into his pockets, and paced the small office. "You have to see things from my perspective, Nyah. I'm trying to run a successful business. While people will always have to have their cars fixed, this is still a competitive field. I have to do what's best for the company."

"And I have to do what's best for me."

"You're going to be hardnosed about this, aren't you?" he groused.

"Damn right." She leaned on his desk and crossed her legs at the ankle. "I already have a case against you with this whole situation."

Jeff let out a strangled sound. "It doesn't call for all of that."

"I think it does. Who told you?"

He sighed. "I'm not sure of her name."

"You're lying."

He frowned.

Nyah picked up a pen and began tapping it on the desk. "I know you, Jeff. You love connections. You try to be overly friendly with everyone, and my guess is that whoever called you was familiar. That's why you believed her. So who was it?"

She could almost see the workings in his mind, him coming to a conclusion. "Mandy Sampson, a woman I understand to be his girlfriend."

For the first time since she arrived, Nyah was at a loss for words. She could say it was a lie because Ethan had told her he wasn't into Mandy like she was him. But then she didn't know him or the kind of character he had. The fact of the matter was he had too much drama going on. Nyah wasn't one to battle it out with skanks, high class or low.

"Whatever she is or isn't to him has nothing to do with you or me," she told her boss. "All I'm saying is the day you think you can run my life, I better be brain dead. So am I looking for another job, or are you getting the hell out of my business?"

She knew looking at him it was hard to say, but at last he muttered, "Fine. I'll see you on Monday."

Nyah nodded. "That's what I thought. Have a good weekend, Jeff." And she flounced out of his office.

Tracy was on her heels before she could get two steps. "So what did he say? What did you say?"

"Down, girl." Nyah chuckled. "We can talk in the car. She led the way to the front of the shop and this time greeted a few clients by name, who in turn called out hers as well. A reference to a recipe one of the women had passed on to her was just the right touch to add when Jeff walked out of his office clearly in a bad mood. Nyah pressed her lips together to hide her smile and hopped in her car. "He'll think twice about telling me who to see, I know that."

"Oh wow, did you hit him?"

Nyah rolled her eyes. "No, I didn't hit him. Not saying I didn't want to. I was so mad, but I got my point across. And you know who told him about me and Ethan?"

"Who?"

Nyah sucked her teeth. "Guess."

"That bitch that was wrapped around him at the club?"

"*Ding, ding!*"

Tracy cursed. "You're kidding. Damn, how low she want to stoop to get her claws in him?"

"Apparently to the floor. I'm not sure I want to deal with all the drama."

Her friend pouted. "Aw, come on, Nyah. He's hot as hell. You can't let Jeff and that bitch run you off. It's all principle now. You have to go out with him."

"Oh I'll do the first date, just like you said, on principle. But after that, I'm not sure. I mean if he'd made it plain to her that he wasn't feeling it between them, she wouldn't have felt like she could get away with trying to mess us up. I don't like men like that, who let women hang on forever just to stroke their ego."

Tracy made a noise of agreement. "Yeah, you're right, and he's so fine, I'm thinking he's used to women throwing themselves naked at his head. Probably loves it."

"Yep, I'm not the one. He's going to learn that real quick."

"I hear you."

Chapter Four

"I like the top," he said in that deep tone that sent shivers down to her toes.

Nyah smiled and lowered her eyes. She wasn't the simpering type, but man did he have her blushing like an idiot. "Thanks. It's nothing special."

"I beg to differ." Ethan had the nerve to reach across the table and brush the backs of his fingers over her bare shoulder. She stifled the tremor but was pretty sure he'd seen it. "As we walked in, I noticed the tattoo on your back. What is it, a bear track?"

"Mm," she agreed. The tattoo was on the back of her right shoulder. She had loved the way it looked—dangerous and powerful. Not to be taken lightly, which was what she liked to think of herself. The design had been her first, and she'd drawn it to give to the artist. "I have just the one, but I plan on getting more. I've heard that it's kind of addictive."

His eyes reflected his understanding although she wondered if he did. Someone in his group might like a classier tattoo, if they liked them at all. Or maybe she was stereotyping him.

"I can think of some interesting places you might get one," he suggested.

"I bet you can." She stuck out her tongue at him and opened her menu. For a few minutes he was silent, until she realized her tongue had captivated him. Goodness, men were easy. But then ever since he'd picked her up for their date, Nyah was aware Ethan had turned on the charm. He had every intention of luring her to his bed, and she had every intention of this being the one and only date they shared.

"For starters I'm going to have the coconut shrimp," she told him as she studied the menu. "You can try some of mine if you want. And then I'll have a black and blue burger with onion rings. Later, I might order a dessert to go."

Ethan's eyebrows lay hidden in the hair tumbling onto his forehead. "Can you handle all that?" His gaze swept her thin figure and returned to her face. "A small thing like you?"

She laughed. "Please, I can handle that and more. I have a big appetite." She patted her belly. Not flat since she wasn't joking about eating a lot, but not bulging either. She'd love to be curvier, but so far it hadn't happened. At twenty-eight, she wasn't holding her breath for a sudden positive change. "Are you intimidated? Can you only handle a salad?"

He scoffed with good nature. "I can handle anything you can and more."

"Bring it," she teased.

Nyah wasn't going to lie to herself. Ethan was big, *really big*, and muscular. Obviously, he didn't overindulge, but it would take a lot to maintain all that male perfection. She wanted to sop him up and lick every part, but she'd already decided. One date and one date only. At first, she'd considered telling him what Mandy did, but then dismissed it. What was the point? He'd make more denials about the woman's importance, which would only irritate her since she still felt like he should have dealt with Mandy. Better to enjoy the night for what it was.

Ethan ordered one of the combos of ribs and seafood, and the conversation turned to other topics. His interest in her background and family surprised her, but she answered easily enough his question about whether she was an only child.

"No, I have four sisters and two brothers," she said.

"Wow, big family."

She shrugged. "Yeah, I guess it was a busy household growing up, and it's a real trip at holidays now with everyone and their kids at my mother's place. I'm somewhere in the middle of them as far as order of birth, and still there whenever we all meet. I have my ways of sticking out."

"Like with your work?" Her shrimp arrived, and he swiped one, munching on it while watching her. She dipped another in sauce and bit into it, considering what he meant by the question.

"My dad was a mechanic and so is one of my brothers," she admitted.

Rather than lick the grease from his fingers as she might have done with the sauce, he used a napkin to clean his hands. The man was refined. How he had bent enough to ask someone like her out—a woman who got dirty as a part of the daily job—she'd never know.

"In other words, they taught you everything you know, so there was no reason to oppose what you do?"

She chuckled. "Uh, yeah, no. I did get my interest in cars and stuff from my father and brother. I loved listening to them discuss the subject and hearing the clanging of tools in our garage, but I wasn't allowed in there. My mother is the prissy type. She wants her girls to be just like her. All of them turned out that way, except me. What I learned about fixing cars I went to school for. I had a lot of head knowledge listening to my father and brother, but my dad whipped my ass the time he caught me tinkering with his stuff."

He reached across the table and touched her hand. "I'm sorry."

She shrugged off the hurt feelings that she hoped weren't reflected in her eyes. "No worries. It taught me to be strong and to forge my own way. One day I want to own my own shop. I've been saving for it. Maybe I could do it with a loan and what I have set aside, but at the same time, I'm a little scared. I've heard of this one woman who made a big success of it. I feel I can do it too, but like you indicated, it's a man's world with mechanics."

"I didn't mean to insinuate…"

"Don't worry about it." She slid the dish of shrimp away and pushed a finger between her lips to suck off the sauce. She knew damn well what she was doing to him when she saw him lean back in his chair, but she couldn't resist.

His eyes narrowed on her. "Why do I feel like you're keeping me at arm's length but toying with me at the same time?"

She offered her best imitation of innocence. "No idea. Maybe you're paranoid." His laugh was deep and rumbling. She liked it and wanted to think of something else funny to make him laugh again. Talking to him came easily— *too* easily. She didn't share her dream with just anyone, especially a stranger. That might be his gift, getting people to open up about themselves.

"So what about you?" she asked. "Any siblings?"

"One sister and brother," he answered. "My sister lives here, but my brother, well, he's a resident of the world, as I like to term it. My parents passed years ago."

Nyah offered an expression of sympathy. "I'm so sorry. I guess the three of you are close since there's just you?"

"Not very."

She tried picking up on the emotions behind his simple words but couldn't gather any clues. "Do you spend holidays with them and your brother flies home? Like Thanksgiving or Christmas?"

"My brother tends to spend his winter holidays in

Aspen or any other place his girlfriend wants to go. And Anne, well, she's not the easiest person to get along with. She's older, so she thinks she is my mother."

Nyah smiled. "Ah, okay. She's lecturing you about settling down?"

"Pretty much."

"I get that from my mother all the time." She rolled her eyes. "If I hear it once more, I'm going to scream. Grandbabies, grandbabies, that's all she chants to me when I visit her. I've thought about moving out of state to get away from them all, but I'm going to admit I love family. When that time comes—*if* it comes—I want at least four so we'll have a crowd at holidays too."

He stroked the skin on the back of her hand, sending chills racing up her arm. "A beautiful woman like you? I'm sure you'll find someone to give them to you before long."

Why did that statement turn her off? No, she knew why. Ethan had spoken with stiffness in his tone. He didn't like where the conversation had gone. Probably wasn't ready to settle down, and he most certainly wasn't offering himself in the capacity of her future husband. And why should he? The thought hadn't entered her mind either. She knew at least in part what Ethan was about—a good time in and out of bed. Nothing more. And his sister could lecture until the cows came home. He wasn't hearing it until he was ready.

"So, what do you want to do after dinner?" he asked.

She let him change the subject from their personal lives. "How about bowling?"

He frowned.

"What? Don't you know how?" she teased.

"Of course I do. Just haven't done it in years." He shrugged. "Okay, sure whatever the lady wants. Let's do it."

They finished up their food, and Ethan left a generous tip. Nyah ran her hand up his arm and then stretched up to her toes to kiss his lips. "Thanks for dinner."

"Any time," he rumbled and swatted her on the ass.

Half hour later, they found the bowling alley, and Nyah was dressed in the very lame, very embarrassing shoes they rented out. "So unattractive," she grumbled.

Ethan snickered. "Hey, I happen to think I look good in these."

"Uh-huh." She snickered. "Okay, I have to choose a ball. I'm not too good at throwing it straight, but I still like it."

When she walked onto the platform of the alley they had been assigned, she laid her hand on a black ball and began rolling it around looking for the holes. Ethan moved up behind her and stilled her hands. "First, you don't just grab any ball. You need one you're comfortable lifting without strain."

With him standing so close behind her and the scent of his soap or cologne or whatever he used going up her nose, she couldn't fully focus on what he said. His hard thigh brushed hers as he reached past to check the various balls. Nyah chewed her lip and took deep breaths. She was so turned on, she could have humped his leg. Instead, she cleared her throat and put space between them.

"Try this one," he said and led her to where she would throw the ball. Nyah didn't want to protest his positioning too much or risk him knowing how he unsettled her. She accepted his arms going around her and let him teach her the proper way to bowl. "You want to move in one fluid motion and move your arm as if the ball is just an extension of your hand. No, don't stiffen on the release. That just causes it to be a gutter ball."

She locked up anyway, not seeing a way to avoid it, and just like he said, her ball went straight to the gutter. Nyah frowned and stomped her foot. The curse she muttered wasn't the least ladylike, and Ethan laughed.

"Try it again."

She got another ball, and this time, he swatted her ass and backed up a few steps. Nyah tried to remember his instructions and how he'd guided her arm from aiming to release. She let it rip with a bit too much force. "Aw, damn," she grumbled.

A laugh that wasn't Ethan's came from her right, and she glanced over to find a black man around her age watching her. "See, if you had a brother teaching you, baby, you'd get it the first time."

Nyah peered at him from head to foot and wasn't impressed. "A brother like who, you?"

"Of course," he told her in a cocky tone that grated. "What you doing with that white boy anyway. He can't offer you anything you need."

Nyah took a step in the fool's direction, but Ethan was there all of a sudden, standing just in front of her and glaring at the man. "Do we have a problem?"

"Yeah, we do," the black guy said, apparently not intimidated by Ethan's size. Nyah moved from behind Ethan. Of course the idiot was bold. He had his boys with him who were laughing at everything he said like hyenas. "I was telling this sexy black goddess that she needs to be with a black prince and not you."

Ethan's eyes blazed, and if the situation wasn't so intense, she could enjoy the deep color. They'd turned all stormy-like. She put her hand on his chest to keep him where he was. "Don't worry about it, Ethan. I can take care of this myself." He was about to protest, but she turned back to the idiot who had too much to say about who she dated. She'd dealt with that crap from her boss. She sure as hell wasn't putting up with it from some stranger who thought she should date him because of the color of his skin. "See that's all y'all's problem as it is, thinking we like that stupid mess calling us goddesses. And for that matter why would a goddess want to stoop to being with a prince?"

The man's mouth closed so fast, his teeth clicked.

"You're not real," she went on. "So not sincere. You think your flattery is going to get you in my bed. You think I'd choose you over him? For what? To sit here with your stupid boys all night while y'all have more fun with each other? No, you'd have left me home, right? Talking about boys' night out? Please, I don't think so. How about you handle your business over there, while I handle mine."

With her last words, she made sure to run her hand up and down Ethan's chest and brushed her ass so hard against his thigh, every one of the guys had to feel it. Behind her she caught the swears from the other group and the fool she'd been arguing with saying she wasn't all that anyway. Nyah didn't even hold back her laugh. She had no issue with dating men of her own race, but not people like him. The way she looked at it, she could date whoever the hell she pleased, and nobody had a right to put their two cents into it. Like it or not.

They left the bowling alley later with no more incidents, and Nyah fanned herself while breathing the cooler air in deep. She felt Ethan's eyes on her and turned to look at him with the grin. "What?"

He shoved his hands into his pockets, and his jeans pulled taut across his package. Even in jeans, he was hot as hell. She wasn't a good judge of whether a man was hung based on how he fit his pants, but looking at Ethan was real nice anyway. Women probably broke a leg just to get his attention. She couldn't say she wasn't tempted herself. But then those amazing eyes were already on her. *Satisfying*.

"You're kind of a hothead, huh?" he asked.

Her eyes widened. "Wow, that's the impression I'm giving of myself? I'm not really. I just like to do me and not have people in my face judging me for it. Seems like the few triggers showed up just for today."

He reached out and teased a cord of her hair. "I'm not turned off in the least. I like your fire. But you said today, not tonight. Anything happen earlier?"

She shrugged and turned away from him. "No."

He caught her hand, keeping her from moving away.

When another tug brought her into his arms, Nyah didn't resist. Flattened against his chest was not a bad thing at all. He ran a finger over her cheek and brought it to her lips.

"I've been wanting to drink from these since I last tasted them," he commented.

"I'm not stopping you."

He crushed her tighter to him and covered her mouth. Nyah moaned and closed her eyes. She was just as hungry for it, maybe more. She strained against him and rose up on her toes. Ethan easily supported her weight, and she felt the strength in his biceps as he held her. Heart pounding in her ears, she almost missed the curses from somewhere nearby. She broke off their kiss with a frown and glanced past Ethan's arm.

What she thought was someone being disgusted by their public display of desire was instead the fool she'd argued with earlier cussing out his car. The hood was raised, and he and all his buddies stood looking under it with dumbfounded expressions. Nyah gave a soft laugh. Life was just too good sometimes.

She was about to walk over there, but Ethan didn't let go. "You're not going to help him, are you?"

"Why not? He's obviously having car trouble and doesn't know what to do. I'm a mechanic, remember?"

He frowned. "And you two had an argument not too long ago."

She tried to read from his expression what he was thinking, whether he was worried about the two of them being jumped in the parking lot of the bowling alley, or what. She didn't think it was fear though. Even in suits, Ethan looked like he could handle himself. He could be worried about her safety, but fighting with rusty bolts and handling heavy car parts had conditioned her arms. She might not have gotten into too many scrapes in her life, but she had it on the good authority of her brother, that she packed a mean right hook. And hell, every man was vulnerable to a kick in the balls, push come to shove.

"I'm like a doctor," she quipped. "I can't see a patient in trouble and not take a look."

She strolled over to the men with Ethan close behind. When they stopped not far from the group, she suppressed a smile at how close Ethan stood to her with a hand possessively laid at her lower back. The man acted like she was about to be attacked. But she did like that he would keep her safe if the need arose.

"What's up?" she asked the group. Heads rose from under the hood. She expected hostility, but the dude's expression showed only annoyance.

"Can't get it started," he grumbled. "Just got it back from the shop, and the damn thing is still overheating. What the fuck?"

"Mind if I take a look?" she offered.

"What would a little thing like you know?"

"Apparently more than you." She walked over and peered under the hood. "I'm guessing you drove it here even while it was overheating, right?"

"I—"

"And you already know you will probably end up

paying twice as much as you would have if you'd just let it cool down."

He mumbled under his breath, and Nyah laughed.

"Cheer up. From the sound of it, the last place you took it screwed up, and they have an obligation to fix it right at no charge. But since they did, I wouldn't trust them to get their hands on my car again if I was you." She snapped her fingers. "Got a rag or something you don't mind getting greasy?"

They scrambled around looking, and someone produced a hand towel. Her suspicion was that he'd had a leaking gasket before, but now it was cracked. Even a lousy mechanic should have warned him about the dangers of continuing to drive with the car overheating.

"She know what she's doing?" she heard the guy ask Ethan.

"Yes, she works as a mechanic." Somehow she thought his voice was tight, but it might be her imagination. He'd asked her out, so he couldn't have that much of an issue with her job.

The black guy laughed. "Guess it's good to have one person wearing the pants in the relationship."

"Do you really want to insult us at a time like this?" Ethan's tone remained calm, but she heard the threat. She suspected he'd drag her off by force to leave the fool stranded if he didn't shut his mouth.

"Yeah, sorry. Name's Lamont." Nyah guessed they shook hands behind her. "So you and her, huh? You don't look like the type to look her way more than just to admire the view, if you know what I mean."

Nyah rolled her eyes. She was aware her ass was pretty much in the air for all of them to see, and her pants were tight. Even her small butt could look good in the right jeans.

"I agree. The view *is* nice. Nyah and I are just having a little fun."

Her lips compressed at his words. He could never have made it plainer. Anything serious between them was impossible, and it wouldn't cross his mind. When she straightened and turned around, the look in Lamont's eyes said he'd come to the same conclusion. Knowing he knew pissed her off even more.

She had handed her purse to Ethan when she began inspecting the engine, and she wiped her greasy fingers on the towel, shaking her head before searching it. "It's just as I thought. Your guy dropped the ball. You can try going back to him, or you can call a friend of mine." She handed him a card. "He'll give you a fair price, and he'll give you documentation that shows the last person didn't know what he was doing. You can see if he'll give you a refund or take him to court if he doesn't."

Lamont took the card with reluctance. "Why not you?"

She grinned. "My shop does dealership work. And here's a number for a tow. You're not going anywhere in that tonight."

"Fuck!" he growled. "Well, thanks anyway. You're okay."

She tossed him the filthy towel, gave a two finger wave,

and walked off. In Ethan's car, she said nothing on the way home. He tried several times to engage her in conversation.

"Something wrong?"

She shrugged. "Not really."

"I know there is. What is it?"

Nyah did her best to hold onto her temper. "Look, don't worry about it. Tonight was fun. Thanks."

"Why does that sound dismissive?"

They drew up to her apartment complex, and Ethan cut the engine. Nyah knew he was waiting for an explanation, but she just didn't feel like giving him one. "I guess I'll see you at the shop sometime."

She tried getting out, but he stopped her with a hand over hers. He leaned across the seats and kissed her. From the first touch, she forgot everything, just being consumed by the lust she felt for him, the desire that rolled off the man in waves. Longing had her squeezing her thighs together and raising her chin as if in submission. He released her hand and rested his on her breast. As before she wasn't wearing a bra, so the flick of his thumb across her nipple made it tighten. They could go so much further, but it was better for her sanity that she stop this now.

Nyah grabbed his hand and pushed it away as she broke the kiss. "Good night."

"Let me come in," he murmured, his voice thick with desire.

She swallowed trying for control. "I don't think that's a good idea."

"Why not?"

"Because you're looking for a good time, and I'm not the one." Crap, she didn't mean to admit that or to sound so bitter about it.

He leaned back to peer into her eyes. She dared hold his gaze so he wouldn't think she was afraid of anything. He didn't seem convinced.

"So you don't want a good time?"

"Don't be flip." She frowned. "You know daggone well what I mean. You're just looking for a bed partner, once or whatever. I'm not. It's as simple as that."

"There's nothing wrong with us being lovers." He tried to take her hand, but she pulled away and pressed close to the door, hands folded over her chest. Ethan wasn't giving up so easily. "If what you're worried about is a one-night stand, I can guarantee I'll want you more than once."

Her eyebrow flicked up. "Oh really? You know that, huh?"

His eyes sparkled. "From the first kiss."

Maybe she should feel flattered…or insulted. One thing was for sure, she was still bothered by him saying they were just having fun. She knew that, but hearing him say it got under her skin. She opened the car door. "Thanks again."

The car door slammed behind her, and she hurried up the walk trying not to look like she was. Everything inside of her wanted to turn and jet back down there into his arms. *No, I made the right decision. Just stick to it, and everything will be fine.* The problem was she didn't believe one word.

Chapter Five

Ethan pulled up to the front entrance of his company and stopped the car. Mandy threw him a confused look. "What are you doing? Aren't you going to park?"

"I have to make a quick run. I'll be back before the meeting."

She rested manicured fingertips on his sleeve. He wasn't sure when he recognized it as a possessive move on her part, but it had never bothered him until today. They had been childhood friends, their parents being golf buddies as far back as he could remember. But after they grew up, he had made it plain to Mandy he had no interest in her. Not that she wasn't beautiful. He'd be a blind fool not to see it with her long hair and perfect figure. However, she was like a sister. Seeing her differently than that didn't seem possible. Besides, he knew her personality better than most. Mandy was a clinger. Every one of her former boyfriends had mentioned it either to her or to him in a desperate attempt to find out how to get free of her. No thanks.

"Where are you going? I can go with you. I don't have much going on this morning," she told him.

He reached across to open her door for her. "It's fine. Thanks."

Without further explanation, she had no choice but to get out, and he ignored the pout. Many men had fallen to her feet with that expression. He'd even given into what she wanted on occasion, but not today.

Seeing he wasn't going to say more, she sighed. "Fine. I'll see you later. Lunch?"

"I have something planned already. Sorry." When she was clear, he slipped sunglasses on his face and roared off down the street.

The flower shop where he intended to buy Nyah a bouquet of roses wasn't far. Something about the woman had him thinking about her nonstop. He wanted her, to touch, to taste, to even listen to her sassy mouth. Nyah was quick-witted, and he didn't think he'd be bored in her company. If dating was what she wanted, then he would do it for now. First, he needed to show her he would not give up so easily.

* * * *

Nyah cleaned her hands the best she could before touching the roses. "That's so sweet of him."

Tracy leaned in and took a huge whiff then sighed with

satisfaction. "You don't like flowers."

"Doesn't stop me from realizing it was a sweet gesture." Nyah had caught Jeff's facial expression the minute he spotted the delivery guy. No one at the shop got flowers delivered. Just wasn't that type of place, and Nyah had stirred quite a bit of interest to her embarrassment. Especially since she wasn't the type to like them. Tracy knew her well. But she had spoken the truth. She appreciated the gift even if she did know that Mr. Ethan Daniels was trying to change her mind about not seeing him.

"Are you going to call him?" Tracy asked.

"Nope."

They sat outside the shop on a bench for their break. The time together at work was rare because they kept so busy. The sun shined without it being overly hot, and a breeze kicked up every now and again. Tracy, always in the middle of quitting, smoked a cigarette and flicked the ashes in the tray next to them. Nyah waved away the smoke and moved her flowers from between them to the other side.

"Why?" her friend grumped as she stood to clear Nyah's air. "You were sweating over that man all this time, and the first chance you get, you let it go. He wasn't all that on the date?"

"He was."

"Ugh, tell me something," Tracy insisted.

Nyah laughed. "He just wants sex. I don't really have a problem with that, but you know how it is. You get connected, start feeling something. Then next thing you know your heart is broken." She stared out at the busy street half a lot away from them. Cars zoomed by, and buses and trucks polluted the air. "To tell the truth, I think even once is risky. I want him. Girl, I'm not going to lie, I want him so bad. But no. I can't. I *won't*."

"Psyche yourself out," she suggested.

"Please, that doesn't work with me." Nyah's cell phone rang, and she hated the grin that spread on her face. The call was from him. *Why oh why*. Maybe it was already too late, and the only thing that could save her was his loss of interest. "Hello?"

"Hey." His deep voice sent chills down her spine as usual. "Did you like the roses?"

"Yes, thanks."

"And the card?"

She pulled the small note from her pocket and reread it. *Looking forward to many more nights like last night. – Ethan.* Even though they hadn't done anything, his message just had that intimacy about it, and he knew damn well what it did to her. She imagined all the things they could have done instead of arguing with some fool at the bowling alley and diagnosing his car afterward. Ethan didn't pretend he was interested in a real relationship, and she respected his honesty as far as that went. But that *was* how far it went.

"I'm glad you had a good time. I did too." She fingered the edge of the card thinking. "Thank you for teaching me."

Tracy's eyes went wide at that. *"Teaching you what?"* she mouthed. Nyah laughed. Dirty minds think alike.

"I'd like to do a lot more instruction than that," he

offered, taking her cue. "In fact, I'm sure you can return the favor."

"Meaning?"

"Show me what you like, what pleases you and gets you hot."

Okay, and they'd just crossed into phone sex. "Listen, my break is up, and I have to get back to work. Thanks for the flowers. Have a great day." She disconnected the call in the middle of whatever he'd been about to say.

"So?" Tracy intoned with impatience.

"So nothing. It's over. I think I was clear enough."

Tracy smirked. "Yeah, don't hold your breath, girlfriend."

Her friend had turned out to be right. Ethan didn't give up. He just kept sending little gifts and more flowers. His notes remained teasing for something more, and the worst of all, the man never left her dreams. Hot, erotic, dreams of the two of them in each other's arms. This wasn't fair. She didn't even get the chance to forget him and go back to her contented life. Her secret toys weren't doing the trick. If anything, they heightened her desire.

On the fifth morning after their first date, she woke up so horny, she was grouchy. By the time she arrived at work to find still another bouquet, she'd had it. She snatched the flowers off the front counter and dumped them in the trash and then yanked her cell phone out of her pocket. Jeff stood behind the counter, and he opened his mouth to say something. Nyah narrowed her eyes at him and held up a finger. He better not say a word. She'd take care of it herself.

Jeff seemed to read how violent she was feeling in her expression, and he backed off. Instead, he turned toward the front door as if ready to greet a customer. They weren't officially open yet, but when the bell dinged from someone entering, she bit off a grunt of annoyance. She'd forgotten to relock the door.

Her fingers flew over the keys on her phone to call Ethan. For some reason it felt more satisfying to punch it out rather than speed dial him. At the same time, Jeff was saying, "Good morning, Mr. Daniels." Nyah froze.

Another phone rang behind her at the same time she heard the connect to Ethan. She spun around in degrees, schooling her face not to show her surprise that he was there. "I thought I heard a knock in the engine," he said. "You always say don't ignore it. Get it checked out right away."

"You're lying—" She bit her tongue and forced a grin. "Can I talk to you outside a second, Mr. Daniels?"

"By all means."

Nyah tightened her lips and followed him outside. She took his arm and fairly dragged him around the side of the building so they were out of sight of everyone else and then dropped his arm to plant her hands on her hips.

"Just what the hell do you think you're doing?" she demanded.

The innocent expression wasn't fooling her. "I said I thought I heard—"

"No you didn't, and that's not what I'm talking about."

She blew out a breath trying to get a grip. "All the flowers and the gifts? Why here at work, so I can't ignore them or so people will keep asking? Are you trying to guilt trip me into seeing you? Because I have to say, that's so not appealing in a man."

He chuckled. The way he leaned against the wall, arms folded over that big chest and suit jacket straining at his biceps had her almost panting. Yeah, he knew what he was doing, but it wasn't guilt-tripping her. *The bastard!*

"If you want me to stop, just say so," he said.

"Oh don't give me that." Nyah sputtered over her words. She didn't know if it was anger or excitement at seeing him again so soon. Before when she had to wait several months between his visits, it was like a special treat, and she had conditioned her mind to stop thinking about him until it was almost time for the next one. This was much worse, and he knew it. "You're going to get me fired sending all those gifts here."

He sobered. "Fair enough. Then I will send them to your apartment."

"Ugh, man, why don't you move on? You can have any woman you want."

She wasn't sure when he'd moved closer to her, but all of a sudden, he blocked out the morning sun. And she didn't mind a bit—well except for not being able to breathe right.

"So you acknowledge that you find me attractive."

"In an ugly sort of way."

They both started laughing at that comment, and he

stroked her cheek. She shivered and turned her head. He didn't pursue her, but for a long moment, he kept his hand raised. She was all kinds of tempted to put her face back into his big palm. *What is this man doing to me?*

"Dinner tonight at my place," he suggested.

"You just want…"

"And why are you so insulted by the prospect?"

She didn't know what to say about that. He was right. The fact that a sexy man with money wanted a woman like her with narrow hips and small breasts should be a huge compliment. If she was honest with herself, she was scared. They were from two different worlds. She didn't own a dress, and he wore suits everyday. But maybe that was the superficial part. After all, he'd gone bowling with her. No, he wasn't asking for a relationship. Skin-deep was as far as this was going anyway. Oh goodness, she was going to do this.

"Dinner," she intoned. "No more flowers. I…kind of don't like them."

When she met his gaze, he appeared shocked.

"Don't like jewelry either," she thought she'd throw in, "except earrings. Big hoop ones."

He stuffed his hands into his pockets. "Good to know."

She chewed her bottom lip. "I'm sorry. I hope I didn't offend you. I never know how to break that to a guy."

"I'm not offended in the least. I admit I've never met a woman who didn't like flowers and jewelry, but it's okay. I'll have to learn what you do like."

There he went again with that thing he did, making

her feel all special with his attention. She pulled herself to her full height and blew out a breath as she started past him. "That won't be necessary. I agreed to dinner, and you agreed to laying off the gifts."

He caught her before she could get past him and whipped her into his arms. "I don't remember agreeing to that."

"But…"

He covered her mouth with his and caressed along her spine with his fingertips. Nyah turned to putty in his embrace. He kissed her lips over and over as if she was some kind of treat, and he moaned barely lifting his head, "I can't get enough of your sweet mouth."

Nyah shook with the impact of his words. She was like a drunk woman and did all she could to drag herself from his arms.

"I have to get to work," she murmured.

"I'll pick you up at six."

She ran a hand through her hair, knowing it was a mess. She'd have to visit the bathroom and straighten things out before starting on the first car. An engine rebuild waited, but all she wanted was to stay where she was and let him keep whispering words like what he'd just said to her. *No, get a grip, Nyah. That's how you lose your heart. It's all physical for him, but not you.*

"Make it seven," she told him, just to feel like she was still in control. Tonight happened to be an early night for her, but he didn't need to know that. "I can follow you to your place in my car from my apartment."

The look he gave her told her the man was not fooled by her manipulations. Ethan had the appearance of being the kind of man who got what he wanted, when he wanted it. Nyah was not sure she was up to the task of defeating him, but she was damn sure going to try.

* * * *

Ethan's apartment was just what she would expect, a penthouse uptown where single men took women they wanted to fuck without strings. The place was for people with a bit more money. Not that she didn't make good money. Of course she did, but saving most of it for her future dream didn't leave much for luxuries like Ethan's apartment.

His oversize kitchen could earn a spread in Better Homes and Gardens, and all the furniture she spotted from the living room to the dining room looked imported. Even the walls were decked out with landscapes. Some were so huge, she was sure he had to hire someone to come in and put them up.

"Nice," she said simply.

Ethan's expression was one of modesty. "Thanks," he murmured. "I just have a few finishing touches to make on dinner, and we can sit down."

She nodded. "So you really are going to feed me?"

He chuckled. "Of course. Don't forget. I've seen your appetite, and I fear for my life if I don't."

Nyah sucked her teeth. "You know you're cold, right?

What, you think I'll eat you?"

His eyes flashed, and the suggestive smile he gave her spoke volumes about who was going to be eating who if he had anything to say about it. Nyah rolled her eyes and walked past him. The swat on her ass told her he already had expectations. She took a stool positioned at the kitchen counter and rested her elbows on the glossy top. "So what will you do if I thank you for the meal and walk out of here leaving you…hanging?"

"That won't happen," he said with confidence. Nyah was about to let irritation take hold before he continued. "I saw it in your eyes that you'd made the decision when I invited you. You strike me as a woman who knows her mind. Coming here wouldn't have happened if you weren't going to go all the way. It was your way of keeping control."

"Okay, dude, don't even psychoanalyze me. Let's just say you might get lucky. I could still change my mind."

He bowed his head in acknowledgement of her prerogative, and Nyah laughed. She liked him a lot, and he knew it. But he wasn't hiding how much he enjoyed her company either. Somehow she didn't think he was playing her. And shoot, how could she fault a man who had come out of the collared shirts and slacks for another T-shirt and jeans. Ethan's ass looked yummy in his pants. She resisted going over and pinching his rear. He might return the favor.

"I can't believe you know how to cook," she commented.

"Anne thought it would help me find a wife." He shrugged.

"Wow, strong-armed you into the kitchen, huh?" She

tried picturing it and failed.

He paused to stir his sauce and gave it a taste. A few more spices went into the pot. Whatever he was cooking smelled incredible. Her stomach stirred with her hunger.

"I was much younger, before my growth spurt," he informed her.

Before the muscle. Nyah tried her best not to lust over the man, but being real with herself, it wasn't happening. He was right. She had decided when he invited her that she'd sleep with him. Her fight hadn't lasted long, but maybe after she'd sated herself with his body, she could put up more of a shield. Then again, his attraction might be all out of his system after that.

"What are we having?" she inquired to take her mind off how much she wanted him.

"Pasta primavera with homemade sauce, French bread, and what type of wine do you like?"

She wrinkled her nose, considering it. "Red wine, I guess. If I'm not having a mixed drink, I usually have a beer. Wine is a rare thing."

"I have beer." He indicated the fridge. "Grab us a couple?"

"Sure." She strolled over to what looked like a double-wide trailer of refrigerators. The thing was commercial quality at least, and when she opened it, her eyes bugged that there was so much food, on every shelf. "Wow, you sure you have enough?"

"Oh that's because I'm frequently the host for company meetings."

"Because you cook, right?"

"Pretty much."

Nyah bit her lip to keep from asking why Miss Mandy didn't cook for him and his associates. Ethan didn't need to start thinking she was jealous of the woman because she wasn't. She just couldn't stand her ass.

They settled in for a dinner that turned out to be delicious. She sat back from the table, full but not stuffed. "Oh man, you're incredible."

"I'd hope to make you say that in a whole other capacity, but thank you."

Nyah rolled her eyes. "You're not going to quit, are you?"

"Why should I?"

She gave in to the teasing. "Yeah, why should you?"

He was about to say something more, when his cell phone rang in the other room. He excused himself to go answer it, and Nyah thought she'd help clean up the dishes. The domestic feeling was stomped mentally under her feet as she loaded the dishwasher. Soon she had the table wiped off and was headed toward the living room when she heard his voice.

"Yes, it turned out great," he was saying. "My company enjoyed it as well."

Nyah hid a smile as she headed past him to take a seat on the couch, but he reached out to grab her and pull her back against him. He wrapped his arm around her waist, pinning her in place. When his hand headed too far south, which made her feel weird with his sister on the phone, she smacked his arm.

"Quit it, Ethan."

She wiggled in his hold and managed to escape but not before she heard his next words and wondered about them.

"What does it matter what race she is?" he snapped. "Yes. Yes, she is. I have to go. I'll call you this weekend. Good-bye."

So his sister had heard her voice and guessed she was black. Ethan had said he'd been with black women before, but maybe his sister didn't know that. Nyah wondered what her reaction was—distaste or disinterest. Well it wasn't disinterest or she wouldn't have asked about her race. Whatever. She was not the type to be moved by people and their small-minded issues except to tell them about themselves if they provoked her.

Ethan joined her on the couch. He took her hand and brought it to his lips to kiss. "About my sister…"

"Don't even worry about it." She ran a hand over his chest and down lower to his stomach. "What she thinks or says doesn't bother me."

His expression showed he was evaluating whether she spoke the truth, and then he seemed to conclude she was. He focused on her hand a second and then smiled at her. "You realize where you're going?"

Her eyebrows went up. "Do you?" she teased. "Need me to spell it out for you?" She rubbed his cock through his pants and felt it respond with a twitch. The longer she stroked, the more it hardened, and the wetness in her panties increased.

"Maybe we should wait until our food has settled a bit," he suggested.

Nyah stood up and climbed onto his lap. This time his hands spasmed on her thighs. "Whatever you want," she quipped.

His gaze went from her eyes, to her lips, on down to her breasts and then to the heat between her legs. "Forget what I said. I want you now."

Chapter Six

Nyah crossed her arms over her waist and grabbed the ends of her T-shirt. She raised it above her head and tossed it aside. "Well?" she asked him, tilting her head a little.

"Just as I thought."

Her eyes grew wide, and she covered her small breasts with her palms. "What?"

Ethan dragged her hands down and pinned them on the tops of her thighs. "Just enough for a man to enjoy himself sucking them." He followed his words with his lips closing over one erect nipple. Nyah sucked in a breath as arrows of need shot to her pussy. She whimpered and closed her eyes. Ethan moaned. He drew back enough to flick the tip of his tongue over the peak and then took it into his mouth once again.

He raised his head, and she protested. "Don't stop."

His eyes blazed. "Do you like it?"

"Yes, of course."

"And what will you give me if I suck your delicious, chocolate nipples?"

She scooted forward on his lap and gyrated her hips. Her pussy ground into his crotch, and she felt him grow harder if that was even possible. Nyah held on with hands at his shoulders while looking into his eyes. "How's this? You want me riding you?"

"That and more." His hands skimmed along her sides, and he brought his thumbs around to the front to play with her nipples. "Your dark skin is tantalizing me. So rich and beautiful, smooth as silk. And you taste..." He lowered his head to kiss her at the valley between her breasts. "You'll stay the night. When I make love to a woman, I enjoy taking my time."

"I have to work tomorrow."

His head came up, and the displeasure was plain in his expression. "Can you call in?"

"I can't."

"Then be prepared to be exhausted tomorrow, because I will take all of you tonight."

Nyah leaned in and kissed him. Just like him, she couldn't get enough of tasting his lips. They were firm, and the bottom one thicker. She liked how it felt between her lips when she sucked on it. The slight salty flavor and the heat ignited her body.

She stood up and unbuttoned her pants. So far he hadn't removed any clothing, and she began to wonder if he hid imperfections. Hell, her body wasn't all that. She had small scars on her lower legs from when she'd been a tomboy growing up. Of course she was too thin, and her boobs weren't as big as she would have loved. But he appeared to like them.

Ethan watched her every movement. His eyes traced her hands as she slid her pants over her hips and pushed them down. She wore white bikini panties, special lacy ones that she'd picked out just for the night. The way he stared, she knew she'd made the right choice.

"Come here," he said and held out his hand. She laid her fingertips in his palm, and his closed over hers to pull her closer. Nyah caught her breath when Ethan hooked a digit into the waistline of her panties and tugged them lower. A rumble of pleasure rose from his throat. "You shave?"

"Wax."

"That surprises me. I thought—"

She put a hand on her hip. "What that I'd be all natural and bushy?"

Another tug had her on the couch at his side, and he put her on her back with him leaning over her. "You're the most beautiful, desirable woman I have ever met."

"You say that to every one of them."

"I mean it more with you," he asserted.

That didn't make her feel better. And then again it did. Recognizing it for a line helped her keep it on a physical level and hold the emotions in check. She offered him a look that said she wasn't falling for it, but Ethan was time enough for her. All thought drifted away on a haze of pleasure when he buried his head between her legs and gave her pussy a good, long lick. Nyah shuddered and raised her hips to meet his mouth, but he moved away and aimed for her belly. She groaned in protest.

"Easy, beautiful," he said. "What did I tell you before? I like to take my loving slow, so it's good for the both of us. I promise you will enjoy yourself."

She ran her hand over his chest and tried undoing a few buttons. "You're not taking your clothes off. Are you shy?"

His brow wrinkled displaying his disgust, and he took her hand away from his shirt and kissed it. "No, all in good time. First, I will please your body with you like this, vulnerable before me and at my mercy."

"You want me under your control. I'm not that easy."

"No?"

Nyah knew where he was headed before he got there, but this time he didn't use his mouth. Ethan pushed a single finger inside her wetness, and it was all she could do not to cry out. All of a sudden, she wanted to prove to him that he didn't command her body, but resisting the sensation of him pumping in and out was tough. The fight grew downright impossible when he added another and another.

Her jaw grew slack, and she shut it, swallowing the moan that rose in her throat. He pressed the heel of his hand against her sensitive folds and applied pressure. Her hips came up off the couch for the second time. *Damn him, that feels good.* But she didn't make a peep out loud.

"Oh, you've decided to resist my touch?" He tsked with his tongue against the roof of his mouth.

She licked her lips and grasped his wrist. "What are you going to do?"

Ethan didn't even try to shake her off. He simply moved his hand and replaced it with his lips. Nyah held onto him, squeezing when his tongue zipped over her clit and then delved between her folds. Her gasp was too noisy and desperate.

"Ethan, don't."

"You don't like what I'm doing? You don't want me to eat your pussy?"

"Oh goodness, why do you have to talk dirty to me?" she moaned. She arched her hips and began pumping against his mouth. He had returned to tasting her without waiting for an answer to his question. The man knew what he did to her. He had to recognize that she was halfway to an orgasm already, but he kept his pace unhurried. Each time she shuddered like she would explode at any moment, he backed off and blew on her clit. Nyah squirmed and whimpered, but she didn't come. Not yet.

Her juices began to flow in earnest, the more excited he got her. As fast as it ran down her snatch, he licked it up, and then he concentrated on her clit, sucking the swollen bud until she was dizzy and jerky in her movements. She wanted more, but then she needed him to stop. One minute she pulled him closer. The next she pushed at his shoulder.

Ethan teased until she screeched and shouted his name. "Please, I beg you, Ethan. I've got to come."

He concentrated the tip of his tongue on one spot at the top of her clit. Somehow that was more sensitive than the rest of the swollen bud, and where seconds before she could muffle her moans, with him laving that spot, she couldn't hold back. Her rocking with his rhythm grew erratic, so he threw a big, muscular arm over her hips to hold her down. Nyah sank into the cushions beneath her. She was his prisoner, unable to do anything except take what he gave.

Ethan took her entire clit into his mouth and sucked so hard, she screamed in delight. Seconds later, her pussy pulsed and core muscles contracted. She shouted a second time, and then her orgasm erupted. She'd been wet before, but the climax was so powerful, that she almost gushed with thick, white liquid. And each squirt, Ethan licked it up and went back for more. He kept at it, laving every drop until she was done and still, breathing hard.

"Now," he said, sitting up. "Wasn't that good?"

She didn't feel the need to argue or pretend. "Yes, so good."

"Want to please me?"

"Of course." She reached for his belt buckle, but he stopped her. "I can't suck you through your clothes."

He shook his head. "No, I'm going to undress for you like you did for me. Lie there or sit up, but watch me."

Nyah didn't move. She couldn't have, but she turned her head as he shifted to his feet. Each button he loosened made her tighten with anticipation. Her breath came in heavy pants, and she trained her eyes on him, not wanting to miss a thing. A tanned, powerful chest came into view, and he slipped his shirt over his shoulders to let it fall to the floor.

"Hey, aren't you supposed to dance or something, sway your hips?" She couldn't help stretching a foot out to rub the front of his pants with her toes. The muscle jumped under her touch.

"Sure. Right after you dance for me."

"Not happening." He grinned and started on his pants. She moaned. "Mm, yes, baby, show Mama what you got."

His eyes widened, and Nyah laughed with a shrug. She felt no shame in admitting how bad she wanted to see. As soon as he was bare, she was going to get her hands on his cock. Ethan let is pants fall, but boxers still blocked her view. She frowned.

"Easy, I'm going to give you what you want." The boxers hit the floor, and Nyah just suppressed a whistle. Just as she thought, Ethan had a nice, big cock. Thick and long, it jutted from his body in invitation. What surprised her was that he didn't have a tan line anywhere. His taut skin, stretched over hard muscle, was smooth in its bronzing to the point of perfection.

"You lay in the sun..." she began.

"In the nude, yes." His eyes challenged her to shocked, but it just confirmed what she already knew. Ethan was confident in every aspect of his life. He didn't question his attractiveness to women in the least. "I have a high privacy fence in my back yard and a pool. Maybe you'll join me sometime."

"Yard? Pool?"

He nodded. "At my other place."

Damn. "In the nude?"

He grinned. "Why not?"

Nyah sat forward and reached for his cock. This time he didn't stop her. She marveled at how broad he was, how her fingertips didn't meet when she held his cock. *Man oh man, he's going to kill me with this.* But she was all for it. She stuck her tongue out and licked the head, dripping with precome. She moaned and went after more, pushing the cap into her mouth. A long, slow suck had Ethan gasping. He knotted his fingers in her hair but didn't push.

"Take it slowly," he instructed. "I don't want to hurt your pretty mouth."

She licked him on the underside all the way down, while enjoying the way he tasted, smelled, and the texture under her tongue. When she reached his balls, she came back up to take him into her mouth again. Sucking and pulling on him with her lips made his cock pulse, and Nyah didn't stop for a long time. Not until he began to protest.

"You're going to make me come, Nyah."

A tremor went through her at his use of her name, but she nudged it away. "I thought that was the point."

"No, when I reach my release, my cock is going to be inside your tight pussy."

Another shiver took her, this one for a whole other reason. She closed her eyes and didn't stop laving his shaft. "You're talking dirty to me again."

"I can do better than that." Before she could protest, he removed himself from her hands and mouth and shifted her so she lay on her back. Nyah's breathless "wait" was ignored as he placed a knee between her thighs to climb over her. He leaned in close to her ear. "I'm going to fuck you so completely, you'll beg me to stop. Your poor little pussy doesn't stand a chance against my assault."

Nyah wanted to squeeze her legs together, but she couldn't with him between them. She swallowed and squirmed. She reached down to rub her clit, but he stopped her and pinned her arm at her side.

"Oh no you don't. That's mine."

She shook so hard, she had to clench her jaw to keep her teeth from chattering. "I want to come again," she managed to push out.

"Not until I'm in you."

He stared into her eyes, and she almost felt like she couldn't look away. They were forgetting something. Ethan dropped closer so his cock head brushed her mound. Nyah's hips rose without her thinking about it, and she keened.

"You're so close." He kissed her chin and then licked her bottom lip. "So hot for me to take you. It might hurt if you've not had a man of my size before. I'm going to take it slow, but I promise in the end you will love it."

"You're pretty sure of yourself." In reality she felt his power like it was a tangible thing. He must have known that he could capture her with one experience. Leaving him alone after this would be tough.

"I'm sure of *you*," he corrected.

His chest grazed her nipples, and she raised the hand he didn't have trapped to touch his shoulder. "We need protection." Thank goodness her mind started to work at last.

He eyed her a few seconds and then sat up. He grabbed his pants and pulled a condom packet from the pocket. Did he have more in there? Man, she hoped so.

Nyah watched him cover his shaft and toss the empty packet on the table. He turned back to her. "Where were we?"

She pointed to her neglected heat. "Right here."

"Mustn't keep it waiting." He leaned in and kissed her and then spread her folds with the fingers of one hand while guiding his cock into her with the other. Nyah sucked in a sharp breath and uttered a small squeak of protest right behind it. She shut her eyes and squeezed his thigh. Ethan made a soothing click with his tongue. "No, baby, don't tense. Relax for me."

How could she? The pain was not bad by any means, but he did stretch her, and she felt a moment of panic when his cock pierced her tight entrance. Ethan pushed her legs higher to open her up, but that made her feel more vulnerable to his command. She fought him a little without thinking, and he went still in an instant.

"Nyah, look at me," he ordered.

She swallowed but didn't open her eyes.

"Nyah." His voice was sharp, so much so that she obeyed without thinking about it.

As soon as her gaze met his, instead of anger or impatience like she expected, she saw gentleness and understanding. A lump thickened her throat, and she tried pushing it down.

"We'll stop right here if you're not ready," he said. "As I said, I don't want to hurt you. That doesn't give me pleasure."

Somehow as he spoke, she calmed down, and her muscles began to relax. He could have pushed in farther with less strain, but he stayed where he was, just a couple inches deep into her pussy. Nyah believed him. She trusted that he would get up off her if she gave him the word, even if it was difficult and he had to deny his body's desires.

She raised her hips so that his cock sank farther. A shudder rocked her to be echoed by one in him. With his shaft seated to the hilt, their pelvises touched, and a sharp jolt of pleasure coursed through her system.

"Do it," she whispered. "I want to feel you pumping in me, Ethan."

He began moving, thrusting in gently and then picked up speed when she didn't cry out in pain. Nyah curled her legs around him, pressing her feet into the backs of his thighs. She moaned and pushed up to him, their hips grinding together.

"Oh, yes, baby, damn it your pussy feels incredible." He captured her lips and pushed his tongue between them. Nyah gave herself up to him, wanting more. When he explored lower to her neck, she arched it to give him full access. "You're so tight, and you taste so good, I can lose myself."

"It should be a crime to be as big as you are. Mm, Ethan don't stop," she pleaded. He was going to ruin her.

She just knew it. No skinny-dick dude could come along after Ethan. Why didn't she listen to the warnings? *Forget that, girl, enjoy it!* "Go deeper, Ethan. Harder, I want you to wear me out."

She didn't have to repeat herself. Ethan seemed to have been waiting for just that. He pounded into her pussy while keeping rigid control so he wouldn't bump her cervix. Nyah's screams of delight had nothing to do with pain. She rode with him as best she could, clutching his shoulders, and gasping because the sensations were too strong.

Her orgasm came out of nowhere, slamming through her core and spreading out until her limbs shook. She keened, crying out his name and lying motionless because she couldn't do anything else. Ethan didn't slow down from grinding inside of her until she'd gone through two or three aftershocks. When she thought she would faint if it didn't ease soon, he grunted and went still. She felt the pulse and knew he had found his release. He wrapped a hand behind her head and held her tight to him while he came. After a few moments, he drew back, and Nyah had no idea why she would feel embarrassed. She buried her face in his chest and cringed when she heard his chuckle.

"Again," he whispered.

She started and looked up into his eyes. "Really?"

He dropped a light kiss on her lips. "Definitely. Are you worn out yet?"

Her embarrassment faded away. "Nope."

"Then I want you again."

She put a fingertip to her lips and gave him a teasing

look. "I hope you have more condoms."

Ethan pulled out of her and rose. She could have wept at the loss, but he shuffled her to her feet. "Bedroom."

Just as they were heading toward it, she heard a *ding* on her cell phone, the one for when she received an instant message. She knew it was Tracy, but she was so not answering that thing—maybe not until morning.

Chapter Seven

Nyah woke but didn't open her eyes. She felt something heavy weighing her down on top but softness beneath her. More hardness at one side. After her foggy mind began to wake up, she figured out what it was. She lay in bed with Ethan where they'd had the most mind-numbing sex in the world, and if she moved an inch, she was sure she'd feel the evidence of it between her legs.

With more alertness, she realized she needed to get out of there. *Get up, Nyah. Open your eyes and go home.* She didn't open her eyes, and not one muscle twitched. Even groaning in annoyance at herself didn't make her move.

Work! I can't give Jeff an excuse to fire me. That did it. She opened her eyes and hefted Ethan's arm off her. She sighed. Being in his embrace had felt wonderful, and she wanted to stay there all day. But risking him waking up and asking her to leave wasn't happening.

She tiptoed back to the living room. After gathering

her clothes, she threw them on and hurried out the door. She would have loved a shower, but taking the time was too risky. Out on the street, she glanced up and down the block to get her bearings and then figured out which way Trade Street lay. She could catch a bus at the terminal and ride back to her side of town.

Her cell phone beeped in her pocket, and she pulled it out. Ignoring the friend request from Facebook, she went to the instant message button and clicked it. Just as she suspected, the message had been from Tracy.

How's the date going? You're not answering? Must be doing the nasty.

Nyah laughed and then groaned. Everything inside her wanted to go back, but she kept walking. The speed dial connected her with Tracy, who was due in today the same time as she was, so Nyah knew she was awake.

"Hey," she said when Tracy answered. "I'm going to be a little late. Cover for me?"

"Uh-huh, I know you not going to leave me hanging and not tell me what happened last night."

Nyah rolled her eyes. "Well, let's just say I'm taking the bus right now."

"What!" Tracy screeched. "That fool didn't take you home? Wait, you're still out? Did you sleep over?"

"If you calm down, I can tell you." Nyah laughed. "There was very little sleeping going on. The man... Oh my goodness, Tracy. Girl, the man is hung, okay? Hung!"

Tracy groaned as if in agony. "I'm so jealous."

"I'll tell you the rest when I get in, on break. I think I

see the bus about to leave, and I'm going to have to run."

"Damn," her friend complained. "Okay, see you then. Oh, are you going to see him again? I have to know at least that."

Nyah bit her lip. "I don't think so. Gotta go." She ended the call and ran for her ride home.

By the time Nyah had showered and changed clothes, she was more awake but no less sore. Her muscles were fine as she bent and pulled and prodded all day long at work. The ache was between her legs, and yet, she could have killed for another round with Ethan. For the entire morning, she couldn't get him out of her head, and what pissed her off most was that he didn't even call. Of course he didn't. She'd done the right thing in leaving on her own. He would have rushed her to get dressed. Maybe he'd have been polite long enough to run her back to her place, but that would have been it. The knowledge still hurt.

"Well easy come, easy go, I guess," she said trying to convince herself.

"So?" Tracy demanded at break.

Nyah sighed. She didn't want to relive everything by sharing what happened, but Tracy was her friend, and she'd never felt the need to hold anything back from her. "It was amazing. Like I told you he's thick and long, and he knew how to use it too. I don't know how many times we had sex, but it was a lot. He has a drive that's out of this world."

"Did he do you in the butt?"

"Tracy!"

"What, I'm just asking." Her friend laughed and bit

into the tuna salad sandwich she'd brought in.

"No, we didn't go that far, but we had oral. You know I don't do that with just any man, but I was so turned on I couldn't help it." She stared at the ground while chewing her own sandwich and remembering every touch and every word. "He talked dirty to me. Oh man, how I love that."

"Then why aren't you going to see him? And why didn't you let him take you home?"

"Both have the same answer. If I let him, I would fall in love. Hell, I wonder if I'm not a little bit already." She shook her head and stood up to toss away her trash. "It's all physical for him. Men can play that game more easily than women in my opinion, and I've never been good at keeping the emotions in check. I can't do it."

"You want to though," Tracy said.

"Yeah, I guess I do." She shrugged. "But he didn't even call to see that I made it home okay. Whatever. That's done. It was an incredible experience, but it's over. Now I need to get back to work. Those spark plugs aren't changing themselves."

Tracy groaned and popped the last of her sandwich in her mouth, speaking around it. "I hear you. A crying shame too."

Nyah figured she was talking about her relationship with Ethan rather than the plugs.

* * * *

Ethan opened his eyes and rolled over in bed. When

he didn't find Nyah there, he frowned. He raised his head to listen and see if she might be in the bathroom, but the apartment seemed suspiciously quiet. He slipped from the bed and searched his place to be sure. She'd left. She'd actually snuck out of his bed and left!

For a moment, he considered rushing back to his room and throwing something on to see if he could catch her, but then he stopped. No, if she'd wanted to be there, she would have stayed, and he would not chase after her to make her do something she didn't want.

As he headed into the shower, he considered all they'd done the night before. He had kept things straight except for the oral sex. Wanting to do so much more had crossed his mind, but he didn't know her well enough to know if she would go for it yet. He had planned to discuss it with her over breakfast.

When he stepped from the steamy bathroom with a towel around his waist, his cell phone caught his eye where he'd left it on the side table. A scan of his messages showed none were from her. Not that he had expected her to call. His thumb paused over the key to phone her, but once again he stopped himself. He paced instead, drumming his fingers on the back of his phone. Why the fuck did she leave? She'd enjoyed last night. He knew she did by the responses he elicited from her sexy body.

He frowned and tossed the phone on the bed while he searched his closet for fresh clothes. He had meetings all day as usual, and Anne wanted him to stop by the family home that evening. Neither he nor his brother had found a use for it, and since Anne and her husband were raising a brood of four kids, the most logical thing had been to let them use it. Ethan enjoyed his penthouse apartment in the city, but he also kept a comfortable rancher in the suburbs. The family home lay in Ballantyne. His day and night were full. After that, he could decide what he wanted to do about Nyah, when his annoyance cooled.

* * * *

Nyah waited for her date to open the door for her as they left the restaurant. He'd already asserted that he would be a perfect gentlemen, but it was getting old, along with his conversation. Somehow she felt like it was all an act. Aside from that, the chemistry between the two of them didn't exist, and if he told her another story about his travels in Timbuktu or whatever country he'd mentioned before her mind wandered, she would throttle him. Of course she enjoyed the thought of traveling to exotic places, but the monotone voice her date told his stories in—when he wasn't muttering so much she couldn't understand a word he said—did not produce excitement in her.

"So what do you think, Nyah?" he asked when they stopped on the sidewalk. "We could go to my place and have a drink."

Are you serious? "Um, I think that might be moving a little fast. How about you take me home and we call it a night?"

He stared at her a minute like he didn't comprehend,

but then he offered her an insincere smile if she'd ever seen one and escorted her back to his car. Her date's name was Kevin, but from the moment she saw his car, she thought of him as just Yugo. The dings in the body were the least of its issues. The engine rattled, and his brakes needed to be dealt with. She supposed she should be impressed the thing still worked since they didn't make it anymore. Nyah didn't want to seem like a snob, so she kept her mouth shut. Some people didn't appreciate being lectured about their vehicles, and she didn't have to save every car she came across. Not that any feelings of rescue for this one rose inside her.

A short time later, they pulled up to her apartment building, and Yugo switched off the engine. "So you inviting me up?"

"No." She saw no reason to elaborate.

He frowned. "What about a drink?"

"No alcohol in the house. I need to go to the grocery store."

"Well how about a glass of water." He reached out to stroke her face, but she ducked the touch. She'd spent all the time she was going to with this fool. He caught her arm when she was about to get out of the car. "You had the steak, and it was expensive. I think I deserve something for that."

Nyah's tone when she spoke turned cold. "Thanks. ouWould you like me to write a check for my half of dinner because I have no problem doing it!"

He didn't even respond but instead jerked her to him.

Nyah struggled so shove him off but didn't succeed before he planted a wet kiss on her lips. She could have vomited on his shirt. "Get your damn hands off me. I don't owe you anything."

When he didn't let go, she balled her fist up and punched him in the jaw as hard as she could. The blow knocked him back against his door, and he growled. "You little bitch."

All semblance of the gentleman left him, and he forced her back to her door, heaving his heavy body over hers. "That's the problem with you women. You want to show off your breasts and wear tight clothes and think a man won't go after what you're offering. I knew I was going to have you when you walked out without a bra on under that blouse. So nice."

"Like hell," she yelled and tried hitting him again. This time he caught her wrist and slammed it on the window. She cried out. Squirming under him to get away did no good. In fact, it seemed to excite him all the more. Bile rose in her throat when she felt his hard-on pressing between her legs. If she didn't get free soon, she was going to be raped.

His door was ripped open, and her date was yanked from the car. Nyah watched in shock as Ethan drove a fist into the loser's mouth. Blood gushed, and Yugo sunk to the ground. Ethan, not having had enough, dragged him up again and punched him a few more times.

"Don't you ever lay a hand on her again," he said with each hit. The last blow bounced Yugo off the side of his car, and he hit the road. Nyah climbed out of the other side and raced around to face Ethan.

"What are you doing here?" she asked him.

He flexed his fingers, checking she supposed for broken skin. As far as she could tell by the streetlights, his knuckles were red. No more damage than that. "I came to see you. I didn't expect to find you just back from a date."

She put her hands on her hips and glared at him. "Not like you called!"

"Were you—" He sighed. "Mind if we take this inside?"

She hesitated and then decided it was better anyway. She glanced over her shoulder at the bastard that attacked her. "Thanks for rescuing me even though I had it." Ethan's expression said he wasn't buying that she could have handled the situation, but the fact that she had to deal with it pissed her off all over again. She walked over to the loser just coming round and punched him again. He swore, and she walked away.

"Don't you think we should call the cops?" Ethan offered when she let him into her apartment.

"No, he's learned his lesson, I think." She stopped considering it. "Maybe I should go back out there and kick him this time, the asshole."

He caught her before she could walk past him. "Hold on. He's got the message, and if he didn't, I'll take care of it."

She looked him in the eyes, liking the protective air, even though they weren't together. "I don't need you to take care of me. It's not like we're regular lovers. I mean you made it abundantly clear that you got what you were after when I didn't hear from you again."

"And you walked out before I was even awake," he snapped back.

"Oh that's your excuse? Please, I don't believe you weren't planning it all along." She stepped back from him and waved her hand. "You can leave any time!"

When she reached out to yank the door open, he grabbed her hand, did some kind of fancy footwork, and had her up against the wall. He moved in close and pressed a knee between her thighs. All the air left Nyah's lungs in a rush. His length against hers was a whole other kind of feeling than what she'd experienced with that bastard outside.

"I came here to apologize for not calling you," he said. Nyah kept her head bowed. She hadn't wanted him to see her resistance crumble from his first touch.

"Oh," she whispered. She looked into his eyes and saw his amusement. The jerk knew the effect he had on her.

"Are you okay now?" he asked, referring to the earlier incident.

She frowned and wiped a hand over her mouth. "Yeah, all except the memory of that fool kissing me."

"I can take care of that." He lifted her chin higher and claimed her lips. He was right. All memory of any kiss other than his left her mind, and the pleasure of his tongue sweeping inside her mouth made her quiver with need. He raised his head. "Better?"

She shrugged, nonchalant. "Getting there."

He chuckled and released her then walked ahead of her into the living room. Nyah had no choice but to follow. She missed his arms around her and his body pressed to hers. "Would you like something to drink?" she offered.

"Thanks." He sat down on her couch.

Nyah liked the setup of her place, and she enjoyed the neighborhood. The money she made in her job allowed her to live where she wanted for the most part, but it was by no means penthouse quality. Still, she wasn't ashamed.

"Any beer?"

"Sure." She brought him a bottle of what she had and made herself a hurricane then sat down next to him. Right away, he reached for her free hand and linked his fingers with hers. Nyah suppressed a shiver of delight. Ethan was all about the seduction, one hundred percent of the time. She wondered if he even knew those tender touches captured a woman's heart as fast as they did her sexual desire. Did he know what he was doing, or did he care? "So it wasn't a one-night stand."

"Of course not. I think I mentioned I already knew I'd want you more than once."

She looked away and took a sip of her drink. "I thought it was just a line to get in my panties."

He released her hand and made her look at him by turning her head. "I never say what I don't mean. You'll learn that about me very quickly, Nyah."

"I'm beginning to see that."

His gaze raked her and lingered on her breasts, and she frowned. "Do you think I was asking to be attacked because I'm dressed like this?"

"Don't you think that for a second. That bastard should have been hauled off to jail." In the light of the apartment she noticed just how huge his fists were when he balled them. "Better yet, I should have pummeled him into the ground."

She placed a hand in the middle of his chest and kissed him. "My hero."

He caressed her cheek. "Nyah, you're beautiful. There's no doubt about that, and I like how daring you are, how strong. I like a sexy woman. Don't let him affect who you are."

"I won't. Thanks. I was just asking." She grinned, warmed at his words. *You're a sap. You know that, right?* she told herself. *This is why you go with safer dudes and not playboys like Ethan.*

"I wanted to ask you about something," he said after a moment.

"What's that?"

"I'm thinking of buying another car. The vehicle I'm interested in is being sold by a private collector in Virginia. He intended to do some work on it to get it road ready, but circumstances prevented him, and now he finds himself having to get rid of it. Would you be interested in taking a look at it once I have it transported here, maybe suggesting what needs to be done?"

"What's the make and model?" He told her, and she almost cooed with excitement. "I'd love to get my hot hands on it. When?" She bit her bottom lip considering it.

"Soon. Are you sure?" He put a finger out and used it to tug her lip from between her teeth. Nyah remembered that her habit turned him on. She told herself not to look, but she glanced down anyway. His cock was swollen in his slacks, which of course made her wet. "I don't want you to feel like I'm using you. I'll pay you well for your services."

Nyah flicked an eyebrow up at him. "That you will, buddy. But I don't feel like you're using me. I'm going to enjoy playing with your new toy."

"Good. Well, I'll give you the details once I have it." He stood up. "Now, I should go."

"Wha—" She blinked up at him. "I thought you were staying."

He pulled her to her feet and dragged her into his arms. A hungry kiss on her lips didn't make her feel better about his intentions of leaving. He ran his hand over her ass and squeezed. Nyah went up on her toes until his hard-on just nudged the top of her pussy. He groaned and pushed her back gently.

He kissed her again, leaving her breathless. "That will have to hold you for now. You were a naughty girl for walking out on me. I promise we'll get together again. Don't see any other men in my absence."

Nyah couldn't believe he put her from him and was striding to the door. She clenched her hands at her sides. "You arrogant son of a bi—"

He stopped in his tracks, and for some reason, it made her cut off the last of the curse. She thought he was going to be angry when he turned, but the intensity in his expression wasn't from being upset. He returned to stand in front of her and caught her chin.

"Make no mistake about it, Nyah. I want you very much, and I'm not leaving because I want to torture you and make you wait for me. I have some business to take care of. In fact, it never ends. My schedule is always tight. Otherwise, I would bend you over this couch, *and* have you in your bed. Tomorrow, we would wake up together and do it all again. Do you understand?"

She coughed to clear her throat and squirmed a little as she stood there. The ache between her legs to be filled with him increased tenfold. "Um, yeah."

"Good." He spanked her lightly and turned to leave.

Nyah wandered behind him and locked the door after he left. For a long while she stood there, forehead against the wood wishing he wasn't so damn busy and willing her heart rate to calm.

Chapter Eight

Tracy pulled up to the office building, which looked like it had been made entirely of glass. Sunlight reflected off the tinted surfaces from ground floor to the top. Nyah's friend whistled. "Damn, so this is where he works?"

"I guess so," Nyah commented. She too peered out the window of Tracy's car, wondering just how many floors this place had.

"Does he own it?"

Nyah shrugged. "Beats me. I know his family has a ton of shares or stocks, or whatever you call it in the company, but I don't know if they control the business."

"But he's getting paid."

"Yeah, any time he has a penthouse suite uptown and a house in the suburbs, he's getting paid." Nyah reached for the door to get out. "Thanks for bringing me. I think he's going to meet me down here. If he doesn't come down in a minute, I'm going to go be nosy."

Tracy laughed. "Go get your man, girl."

"He's not my man. I think he'd decided we'll be lovers for the time being." She rolled her eyes. "When I get my head together, I'm going to be the one to roll out."

"Uh-huh." Tracy's lips turned up with her disbelief. "Y'all be married by next year."

"Don't say that!" Nyah jumped from the car and slammed the door before jetting around to the curb. All the way, she heard Tracy's laughter following her, even though she had the windows rolled up. Nyah did not need to hear the word marriage. Then she'd be getting ideas. The *wrong* ones that would get her in trouble.

She strolled into the lobby and glanced around. Executives and other office types in suits or business casual walked to and fro as if on the way to an important meeting. She didn't spot Ethan anywhere in the small crowd, so she chose a seating area nicer than her living room to sit down and wait for him.

Each time a bell dinged, she looked over to see if he stepped off the elevator. Twice she'd phoned him and got his voice mail. She stood. "Okay, buddy, this is my off day, and I'm not waiting the whole thing on you."

Annoyed, she stomped over to the guard's desk and gave the sour-faced man behind the desk a smile. "Excuse me, do you know which floor I can find Ethan Daniels on?"

Without answering her smile, the man glanced down and searched the directory on his computer screen. "Director of Finance. That would be the fourth floor, but you have to have an appointment to see him."

Shouldn't he have known who the head of the finance department was? And damn, the head of finance? He was someone important just as she thought. No wonder the man never got a break. Their lives were as different as night and day.

"He's expecting me," she assured him.

The guard looked doubtful, which of course pissed her off. What was with the attitude?

"I'll have to call up and check with his secretary," he said.

Nyah sighed and nodded.

"Ms. Sampson, I have someone here who…"

Nyah frowned. Where had she heard that name before? Sampson. Her eyes widened, and she gasped. *Oh hell no!* Mandy Sampson was Ethan's secretary! And now the guard was telling her that Nyah was downstairs in the lobby waiting for him. That was just great. Now she knew if the annoying man hadn't forgotten she was coming to pick up the car he needed her to look at, then Mandy sure as hell wasn't going to tell him.

"Okay, thank you," the guard was saying. He hung up the phone and looked at her. "Ms. Sampson will be down."

"Is that *Mandy* Sampson?" she asked to be sure.

"Yes."

Still, she wasn't anybody special, but she bet any amount of money, Mandy would come down there acting all high and mighty like Nyah was the hired help or something.

The elevator dinged a few minutes later, and there she

was, wearing a grey skirt that molded her figure and didn't stretch past midthigh. Her heels were too damn high for the office, in Nyah's opinion, but that was for Ethan to call her on. Maybe he liked the view those long legs gave. Nyah swallowed the jealousy, but her old feelings bubbled to the surface. If Ethan didn't like the way Mandy acted with him, then he should have put her in her place long ago.

"Ms. Jones?" Mandy said with a smile on her face. Nyah had to admit it was more of a relief than the stone-face the guard had presented. "I thought that was you. I didn't know your last name since I've only seen your nametag on your overalls at the repair shop."

No she didn't just yell that for the entire lobby to hear. Several heads turned in their direction as Mandy glided up in her sultry pussycat way. The appreciative glances she got with her long hair and big boobs wasn't missed on either of their parts. Especially with the triumphant glow in Mandy's eyes. Nyah wasn't wearing overalls today, but she was dressed down in preparation for working on Ethan's car. She should have known better.

"I'm here to see Ethan," she interrupted before the woman could go on. "Any idea when he'll be down?"

Mandy's perfectly formed brows lowered. "Oh, no, I'm sure he's booked up for the rest of the afternoon." While she spoke she pulled out her cell phone and seemed to be checking the calendar. "Yeah, there's no way. He has important people he's meeting with the rest of the day."

As if to say Nyah herself wasn't important. "Look, this is a personal matter between—"

Mandy held up her finger, still flashing that fake smile. "Let me call him to double-check."

That offer surprised Nyah. She didn't expect such generosity from the woman. "I've already tried—"

"Ethan," Mandy cooed into her phone. "I knew *I* more than anyone could reach you at any time. Listen, I have an unexpected visitor here who…"

Nyah gritted her teeth and clenched her hands so tight, her nails bit into her palms. She was trying to keep it together, especially with the evil guard staring at her as if he expected her to attack Mandy at any second. Who the hell did this chick think she was? At the end of her rope, Nyah stepped forward and nabbed the phone from Mandy's fingers. The guard stood. Nyah ignored him and turned away from both of them as she spoke into Mandy's phone.

"I'm doing you a favor, Ethan. If you can't get your ass down here on time or answer my call, then fuck you, and fuck your stupid secretary. I'm leaving."

She tossed the phone in Mandy's general direction and heard it hit the floor as she stomped toward the exit. The angry yelp didn't mean a thing to her as she pushed the door to the street open and left the building. She should have known better, damn it!

At the end of the street, she paused to wait for the light to change. In the distance, she thought she heard someone calling her name, but she didn't turn around. The walk signal flashed, and she stepped forward, but a man crossing in her direction moved in her path.

"Move it or lose it," she bit out. "I'm not in the mood."

The grin revealed straight teeth in the face of a man who wasn't handsome but gave off a friendly air. Probably fake too. "Sorry, beautiful, but my buddy Ethan signaled me to stop you. He's not only my friend but my boss as well. Can't disobey. Now why don't we see what he wants, shall we?"

Nyah glared up at him. Another man in a suit who thought she was less than him. She knew it was wrong to judge him that way when she didn't know him, but she was still angry. The guy was big though, and it didn't look like she could get by without a struggle. She grunted. "Fine, whatever."

She rolled her eyes when he touched the lower part of her back with his hand, and she didn't miss the glance at her chest. Men were all pigs. They walked along the street until they met up with Ethan. Nyah was thrown a little at the glare Ethan directed at his friend, until the guy dropped his hand from her back. She was tempted to flirt with the man and thank him way warmer than necessary, but her mood was too dark to even try.

"Thanks, Luke," Ethan said pointedly.

Luke got the message. "Any time, boss." He grinned at Nyah once more and then was gone. Nyah turned to go, but Ethan caught her arm and pulled her gently around to face him.

"Come with me, please," he said, but she jerked away.

"I said I'm leaving!" She yelled it and didn't care who looked their way. To his credit, Ethan didn't appear to give a damn either. His gaze never left her face, which pissed her off for no reason. "Let me go, Ethan."

"Nyah, I want you to meet the president of my company."

"Wha—" she squeaked. "Why?"

"Because I want you to see the man who dragged me into a meeting that was not on my schedule and that had little to do with me directly. I want him to see why I stood up and left in the middle of his presentation after you cursed me out on the phone."

Her eyes grew wide. "Oh hell. You're not going to get fired, are you?"

He smiled, and she noticed for the first time that he seemed tired. His beautiful eyes were duller than usual. They were running him ragged.

"No, I won't get fired, but I will get an earful. I'm sorry for making you wait. I honestly didn't mean to."

"You keep saying stuff like that, but still you disrespect me," she complained. "I've cut men out of my life for less."

"Then I'm happy I'm special." He pulled her close, and she thought he was about to kiss her right there on the street with some of his coworkers liable to be strolling along at that moment.

She put her hands on his chest trying to get space between them. He wasn't having it. "I'm a little confused about whether you're an employee or the owner of the company. Nobody would do what you just did and risk their livelihood. Not in this economy."

He kissed the tip of her nose when she wouldn't offer

her lips. "I have quite a few shares in the company—not controlling interest. A long time ago my great-uncle started the place from the ground. Over the years, he did what he had to, to keep it going, including selling off quite a large portion. However, yes, because of who I am, I'm afforded some leeway in what I do."

She wriggled from his arms and started back toward his office. "So in other words I shouldn't be impressed with your walk out?" She tried suppressing her smile. At first Ethan appeared alarmed that she thought what he did didn't mean anything, and then he caught her grin.

"Shall I curse the president for you?" He moved up beside her and tweaked a lock of her hair.

"Uh, yeah, no, I'm good. Thanks."

They laughed together.

"I realize you're busy, Ethan. I can see it in your face, and we're not exactly...I just want you to recognize my side of it."

He nodded. "I do. And I'm going to make it up to you. Dinner tonight."

She patted his cheek. "Sorry, baby, I'm busy with a few things." His eyebrows shot up. "Did you forget the car? Me and her have a date, and you're not invited."

"Her, huh?"

"Yeah, her."

"I have the keys here. We'll go down to the garage where I have it parked." This time in the parking garage, he didn't let her put him off when he took her into his arms. His mouth descended on hers, and he took what he wanted, leaving her weak and needy. When he set her from him, she had to lean on the car for support. The man knew how to get a woman wet, and he'd done it on purpose. Probably to get back at her for how she spoke to him, the bastard. Nyah ran a thumb over her lips to clean them up after the sexy kiss and glared at him. Ethan just smiled like he was innocent. *Not since you were born, I bet.*

"It's going to take me a few days. I only have today off, and then a few hours each night after work."

He frowned. "Don't overwork yourself. I can wait."

"I won't. I love what I do." She blew him a kiss and hopped behind the wheel of the car. The vehicle started easily enough, but her trained ears heard the low *ping* that said he might have some issues. After she'd done her diagnostic, she would let him know about the cost of parts and labor. Ethan had been generous in his offer for compensating her, promising to double whatever her regular rate was. Nyah had turned him down, but he insisted. Either way, her enjoyment would be in getting the old model car going strong and the challenge the project would present. From the looks of things so far, there wasn't a whole lot to do. "I'll call you later."

She drove off before he could answer and zoomed out of the garage with her heart going ninety miles a minute. Nyah might have presented him with a calm exterior, but in reality Ethan shook her to her core every time she was around him. She kept saying they weren't a couple—or hinting at it—but he never responded. She didn't quite know where she stood, or didn't want to know. Every sense said cut it off before it was too late. She couldn't and wouldn't obey. Sooner or later, the truth had to be faced.

* * * *

Nyah wiped grease from her fingers on an already soiled towel and gave the car one last look over. The job was done. She was proud of herself. The work had gone smoothly for the most part, except for a few bumps. Ethan would be happy with the results. She'd done most of the job at a buddy's garage, and that only made her hungrier to get her own shop. Still, she felt satisfied.

After her hands were as clean as they were going to get for the moment, she pulled out her cell to dial Ethan. He picked up on the first ring, and she laughed under her breath. Can't say the man didn't learn his lesson.

"Hey, Ethan," she said. Somehow she always wanted to call him baby but refrained. "I'm all done. You're going to love the customization I gave this puppy. When do you want me to deliver it?"

He hesitated, and she wondered what was going on. "Do you mind bringing it out to my family home?"

"Tonight?"

"Sure. I'm going to be away on business tomorrow, and I can't wait to see you…it." He wasn't fooling anyone. He meant to say her, and the seducing tone to his voice let her know exactly what he had in mind.

"I can drop it off, but then I have to go home and get cleaned up. I worked from a friend's garage."

"Okay, I'll give you directions, and you can call me when you're at the gate. I'll buzz you in and meet you out front."

Gate? Damn, just where is his family home? "Okay, that's fine. See you soon."

Nyah punched in the address he gave with the directions in mind into her cell phone's GPS and started out. Not too long later, she pulled up to some wrought iron gates, and beyond them was a frickin' mansion. Nyah's eyes bugged. Was he serious? The circle driveway was lined with cars, and she frowned. He was having a party…No, wait. His sister and her family lived here, so she was having a party. Nyah glanced down at her ratty T-shirt and faded jeans. A tear in the thigh let her skin peek through where she'd caught it on some equipment earlier. She sighed. Well, she told him she was a mess. He better come outside like he said he would.

She rang his cell. "I'm here. You coming out?"

"Yes, one second."

She heard female voices in the background and gritted her teeth. The gates opened on their own, and she drove through. The drive was wide enough that she could circle around toward the front door. A side road led to what looked like a six-car garage. Four sweet vehicles—newer models—were already in there, but there was a spot for this one if that's where Ethan intended to store it.

When she cut the engine and stepped out, laughter wafted on the evening breeze, and she glanced up to find a balcony expanded across a good portion of the front of the mansion. People milled about up there holding wine glasses and chatting with each other. Everyone was formally dressed in suits and fancy dresses. Nyah had never felt so dowdy in her life. Still, she squared her shoulders and dared anyone to look down on her.

Before she had a chance to call him once again, Ethan was at the door, looking sexy as hell in a dark suit that had to be tailor made the way it snuggled his broad shoulders. He wore subtle cologne that enveloped her in a haze of longing when he drew near.

"Hello," he murmured in that panty-wetting tone. "You found the place okay? Didn't get lost?"

"No, unlike many women, I have a great sense of direction. I never get lost." She looked past him at the door he'd left open a crack. The place was wall-to-wall from the looks of it. "Having a party?"

He shrugged, a look of longsuffering on his handsome face. "My sister. She loves socializing, and once in a while, I can't get out of attending. Tonight is one of those nights."

"Oh the hardships," she teased. "Well I won't hold you up. Do taxis come out here?"

He frowned. "You don't think I'm going to put you in a taxi, do you? What kind of man do you take me for, Nyah?" She didn't answer. He caught her wrist and tugged her gently closer but not into his arms. "Come inside. Have a drink or two, and I'll take you home later."

"Are you serious, man? Have you seen the way I'm dressed? And I haven't even washed all the gook off my skin. I must smell a fright too." She shook her head and took a step back. "It's fine. I don't need a ride, and I won't think less of you if you let me go."

Right at the end of her little spiel, the door to his family's home opened, and there stood Ms. Thing, Mandy, in a dress so short her cootchie must be catching a chill in the night air. "Ethan," she whined prettily, "where did you get to. Oh…" She blinked at Nyah as if she was some odd creature she'd never seen before and couldn't identify.

Mandy came down off the two brick steps outside the door and sidled up next to Ethan, taking his arm. "Everyone's asking where you disappeared to. Anne wanted you to settle a debate we're all having."

Nyah didn't miss the way Mandy ignored her like she didn't exist. The bitch needed to be brought down a peg or two, and the way Ethan's mouth tightened, she could tell the woman was annoying him acting like that. If Mandy wanted him so badly, she should at least learn to read his nonverbal cues.

"Mandy, you remember Nyah," he said as a way to allow her to make it right.

Mandy's eyes widened like she'd just spotted Nyah for the first time. "Oh, the little mechanic." Her gaze shifted to the car behind Nyah, and she laid a hand on her chest. Okay, the dress was made of less material than she'd originally thought. The cut at the neckline was just short of her nipples. "You're here to deliver his car. Okay, now I get it."

"Like you had to," Nyah quipped. She grinned. "Yes, Mandy, okay, the *secretary*." She snapped her fingers and then brought a heavy hand down on the woman's shoulder. "Good to see you again."

When she drew her hand away, the white dress at the shoulder was no longer white. A distinct dark handprint, with fingers curling to her back, was outlined. Mandy's mouth dropped open, and she let out a small squeak.

"You bitch!" she screamed.

"Oh, my bad," Nyah said.

"You did that on purpose." Mandy took a step in her direction, but Ethan blocked her advance. He grasped her arms and turned her toward the house.

"Mandy, I'm sure it will be fine. Try to get the stain out in the bathroom," he instructed. "If it doesn't come out, I'll be happy to foot the cost of a new dress."

Mandy milked his attention, sniffling as she walked to the door. Ethan glanced back at her. "Nyah, did you really have to go that far? I know you two don't get along…"

"You know I think I will come inside." She moved past him and jogged up the steps and into the foyer. The waterfall trickling down one wall that led to the second floor took her breath away, but then she spotted a servant or somebody carrying a try of glasses of wine. She nabbed one and took a huge gulp. Swallowing it down, she scanned the area. A wide archway led to a living room to the left, and on the right was a smaller room with a grand piano and a smaller doorway to another room.

"Bathroom?" she asked the server before he could disappear.

His gaze swept her, but he kept his expression neutral.

"Third door on the right."

"Thanks." Nyah finished the wine and set the glass back on the tray. Then she headed down the hall. If Ethan was only being polite, then he should have kept his mouth shut. Now that she was here, she was going to see how the other half lived. She was not poor by any means, but she didn't have it like this either.

In the bathroom, she didn't linger, but scrubbed her hands until they had a red tone beneath the brown of her skin. She felt pretty sure if she touched anyone now, no grime would be transferred. The clothes would have to do. She glanced in the mirror and combed fingers through her hair. The waves were good, and they hung to her shoulders in reasonable order.

When she left the bathroom, Nyah was surprised to catch Ethan's friend heading up into what she thought of as the piano room. He paused when he saw her and grinned. "It's you, beautiful. What are you doing?" He crossed over to her and took her hand. "Never mind. Come with me."

Nyah opened her mouth to answer, but he pulled her along. Before she knew it, she was in the room standing at the man's side while they listened to someone playing Beethoven of all tunes on the piano.

"Wow," she said. "This is some party."

"Stiff isn't it?" he whispered in her ear and winked. She liked him. He was fun. The amusement on his face said he knew what else she was thinking. "You can't remember my name, can you? I am hurt. But I will let you off because Ethan didn't exactly introduce us."

"Uh, sorry." She laughed. Hey, if he didn't care, why should she. "So what is it?"

He stuck his hand out, and she took it. "Luke. We met on the street when I manhandled you."

Nyah laughed. "I remember. You said he's your boss. What do you do?"

He frowned. "I'm a financial analyst. In other words, I push papers around and stare at numbers all day. Very boring, right?"

"Pretty much," she agreed.

He waggled a finger at her laughing. "I like you, very honest and direct. That's something you don't find in this crowd much. And a lot like Ethan."

She wanted to ask him what else he knew about Ethan, but thought better of it. Besides, she didn't want him to know how into his boss she was. "Aside from your job, I find you interesting."

"I'm in love." He linked his arm with hers, and they began strolling from area to area. Nyah discovered there was a lot more to the house than what she'd seen so far. "Ethan and I hail back to our high school days and then later in college. I was the charity case at our private school. He was the golden boy. Or whatever the dark-haired equivalent might be."

"Demon?" she suggested, and they both had a good laugh.

Across the room, Nyah spotted Ethan, and his attention was locked on the two of them. Tonight, she noticed Luke didn't quickly remove his touch, and she wondered if it had to do with the amount of wine he'd had. For herself Nyah was pissed that he'd defend the bitch rather than her in that incident outside. She knew the situation hadn't warranted ruining what must have been an expensive dress, but it was the principle of the matter.

"Ah, the queen herself," Luke said, and Nyah looked around into the cold eyes of a woman who couldn't be anyone else other than Ethan's older sister. She held herself like a queen, all stiff and nose in the air. Her dress while quality at a glance, didn't reveal even a little cleavage or extra thigh. Where Ethan was built, she was slender, but she did have the height that must run in the family. She appeared to be in her mid-forties.

Anne glided over with a small entourage of women who weren't as strikingly beautiful as she was. Of course not. That would make her less of the centerpiece. "Luke, who is this?"

Luke smiled. "Anne, this is Nyah, Ethan's chocolate bunny. Isn't she delicious?"

Okay, now Nyah didn't know if Luke was gay, just being silly, or wanted to provoke Anne."

"Hello," Nyah said, trying to get Luke to stop the madness, "nice to meet you."

Anne nodded. "And you." Her harsh gaze assessed Nyah, and then she looked over to Ethan. Nyah followed her line of sight and realized Ethan was making his way there. At some point the crowd in the room had thickened. Anne turned back to Nyah. "I can't help asking, don't you own a bra?"

See this is why I shouldn't be out in public—because people goad me.

She tilted her head to the side and grinned. "Do you ever take that stick out of your ass?"

Gasps went up in every direction, and a few outright laughed, including Luke. Anne's entire head went red, and pink tinged the cheeks of her girlfriends. "How could you say such a thing?" one of them snapped.

"Same way she said what she did," Nyah countered.

Nyah couldn't say more than that because Ethan arrived at her side and took a firm hold of her arm. This time he glared at his sister. "Anne, this isn't the place or the time."

His sister sucked her teeth, which surprised her in that it was ill-mannered. She seemed more like the type to point out that it wasn't ladylike or something. "I heard about what she did to poor Mandy. Do you really think this is the environment for your...your..."

"Anne." Ethan's tone had turned icy, more so than his sister had displayed moments ago. Anne's teeth snapped together so fast, they clicked audibly. She spun on her heel and moved away in regal strides with her group following. Ethan looked down at Nyah. "I'm sorry."

She wondered what he was apologizing for, whether it was thinking she could fit in here or for his sister's rudeness.

"We can leave now," Ethan said. "I'll drive you home."

"No way. She's just the thing to liven up this dead party Anne is famous for." The man who spoke pumped her hand. "George Coffers. Do you dance...?"

"Nyah," she supplied and laughed. "I've been known to do my thing from time to time."

Confusion colored his face at her "do my thing" expression, but then he figured out the answer was yes, she danced. "Change that music," he called to no one in particular.

Nyah hesitated, but Ethan didn't protest. Anne would blow a gasket, but that pushed Nyah all the more into changing this party up a little. Someone flipped the stereo from the classic music CD to the radio and scanned the stations. "Right there," she told Luke when she noticed he was the one controlling it. A beat she was familiar with blared throughout the house. Anne must have had speakers in every room hooked into the stereo system. Wherever she was, she must be fuming. Nyah burst out laughing and took to the floor with George.

Partner after partner edged out each other to dance with her, and she found herself teaching these rich folks how to move their bodies to the beat. At one point, a group of women she would never have thought would look her way let alone take lessons from her were gathered around. Everything Nyah did, they copied, and she had them all laughing and having a good time.

At one point, winded, she waved them on, and they danced together. She glanced around for Ethan thinking he'd be angry, but he watched her from a corner where he leaned against the wall. She took a minute to read his expression and discovered it was attraction. Nyah wasn't like any woman he'd known, she bet, and he didn't find that to be a bad thing. The feeling probably wouldn't transfer to love because that was for the movies, but she was okay with it. For the first time since they met, she didn't feel like fighting him off to protect herself.

He raised the glass he held in his hand, and she could kill for something to wet her dry throat. A server passed, and Ethan grabbed another glass and started toward her. Nyah shifted her gaze to the right. Mandy was just entering the room in a different outfit than the one she'd been wearing earlier—still sexy, still way too revealing. She called to Ethan being within arms reach of him, but Ethan kept walking toward Nyah. Nyah suppressed a laugh when Mandy's wide eyes turned from Ethan to her, and she realized she had been ignored. The glare of dislike transforming her beautiful face was priceless.

"I bet you're thirsty after dancing with every man here?" Ethan said, offering the glass.

"Not every one," she quipped. "You jealous?"

He kissed her neck in front of everyone, which shocked her. "Of course. You belong to me, and I don't like sharing."

"Mm," she moaned, standing so close to him, she felt the warmth from his body. A sip of the wine wet her palette but didn't calm the brewing desire starting to build inside. "Well, none of them compare to you, so you have nothing to worry about."

An old song came on the radio "No Diggity." Nyah snapped her fingers and began swaying her hips. Ethan's eyes darkened, and he drifted behind her. They moved together as they'd done that first night in the bar. She looked up at him over her shoulder, and he stared back as if she was the only woman in the place. No, as if she was the single other person in existence. Nyah's breath came in short spurts, and her lips parted. Ethan's head lowered, but he didn't kiss her. Just the heat of their mouths so close was mind-blowing. Her drenched pussy seemed to plead for attention. Ethan placed an arm around her and rested his big palm over her belly. They rocked side to side, and when the song shifted to the female rapping, Nyah pushed her ass out then rotated her hips. She was too short to grind into his crotch, but the way the catcalls rose, it had the same affect with her rubbing into Ethan's thighs.

"Give me a turn with her," someone said.

"Get lost," Ethan growled.

Nyah laughed.

And then the music stopped. Every head swiveled toward the stereo. Anne, still red-faced, narrowed her eyes at Nyah. They were so like Ethan's and yet not the same effect. Why she found it necessary to blame Nyah like she'd made these people enjoy themselves, she didn't know. She could get over it.

Anne switched the music back to the classical CD, and people drifted away, almost like it tamed the natural wildness inside. Nyah shrugged.

"Hey," Ethan whispered in her ear, "let's go somewhere quieter."

She followed him as they weaved through the crowd and up the stairs. Somewhere nearby she picked up voices and figured it came from the balcony she'd spotted from the driveway. Ethan didn't take that route but turned in the opposite direction. He opened a door and stood aside to allow Nyah to precede him into the room.

"This is where I slept growing up."

Nyah let out a whistle. "Damn, this is bigger than my apartment."

He chuckled. "That's an exaggeration."

"Not by much."

On one wall a shelf held trophies, and on another were football pendants, a jersey, and posters. Behind the twin-size bed was a built-in bookcase that had been constructed around the headboard. From floor to ceiling, every spot was taken up with thick tomes. She moved to take a closer look. "Economics and accounting. Wow, you were into the numbers even then, huh?"

"You sound like you can fall asleep just saying it."

She wrinkled her nose at him. "You read my mind." She laughed at his feigned hurt expression. "Sorry. Hey, I'm not knocking you for what you like. And football too, I'm guessing."

"Mm, high school and college." He pushed his hands into his pockets. So sexy given he still wore his jacket. She'd been telling the truth when she told him none of those men downstairs could hold a candle to him. Ethan was what women fantasized about, the strong sexy type that could sweep a woman off her feet.

"The quarterback?" she asked.

"Clichéd. That was Luke. In fact, it's how we met.

Even though he also majored in accounting, he tended to focus one hundred percent on his studies. He was there at my school on a scholarship, so he took it seriously. When the coach found out he could play, he hounded him and even got him extra funding to motivate him. It worked, and I was the guy who protected him against the opposing team."

Interesting story, but she was more interested in what Ethan was like back then. She tried picturing him younger and imagined the cool kid that everybody wanted to hang with. But he'd already said her assumptions were clichéd like in movies. She walked over to him and put her arms around his waist. He kissed her lips, and she parted them to invite his tongue in. He took the offering, and they hungrily tasted each other, moaning and pushing tighter. Nyah's panties were soaked, she knew, and Ethan's hard cock pressed into her belly.

She broke the kiss before they could go too far. "You were the popular type though, right? Easy to make friends. Probably had the head cheerleader throwing herself at your head."

He grinned. "No, not the head cheerleader."

From his brief frown, she had a feeling that if it wasn't her then it was someone. Mandy. He'd mentioned they were childhood friends. For a moment, Nyah experienced what Ethan must have downstairs with so many men vying for her attention—jealousy. But she had him now, even if it was temporary.

"Luke's your best friend?" she asked, wanting to change

the subject away from other women.

He nodded. "Yes. I think of him as a brother since I'm not as close to my real one."

"Oh, I forgot you said you have a brother." She looked past him toward the door. "Is he here tonight?"

"No." Ethan caught her chin and made her look at him. "Tell me you want me to fuck you until we're both exhausted."

Nyah shivered. "Here and now?" He nodded.

She pretended to consider it. "You know how you get me worked up. I might scream your name so loud, Anne will hear, and I can't be responsible for her reaction."

He threw his head back and laughed. She loved watching him.

"Is that so?"

She held up her hands as if it was inevitable. "Pretty much."

Nyah let out a small squeak of surprise when he lifted her in his arms and carried her across the room to lay her on the bed. He followed her down, stretching his length beside her. "Then I accept the risk. I want to be inside of you." He traced a finger down her belly and pointed to her mound. "Here."

Who was Nyah to tell him no?

Chapter Nine

"I want you to fuck me until we're both exhausted," she said, a challenge in her eyes. She sat up from the bed and turned to stand in front of him. After pulling her T-shirt over her head, she threw it on the floor and rested her hands on her hips.

Ethan licked his lips. "Never wear a bra!"

She laughed. "I guess you like my little girls, then."

"Woman, I could suck on those nipples all night long and not be done. I enjoy watching them and fondling them when you're riding my cock." He drew her closer to him and ran the tip of his tongue over her hot skin on up to one nipple. Nyah drew in a breath. She raised a knee to set on the bed beside his thigh, but Ethan kept her in front of him. He seemed eager to feast his eyes on her naked body, and it turned her on all the more knowing how attracted he was.

"What about you? I want to see more of you too." She

reached for his jacket, but he caught her hands and shook his head.

"I liked watching you dance. Your hips are mesmerizing," he said.

She gave a little wiggle to tease him. Just as he said, he watched, hardly daring to blink.

"I want you to do it for me naked."

"Now?" She wasn't down on herself, but just like everyone else, she wasn't that confident about her parts either. Letting it all lay bare and then shaking it around, well that was more than she'd ever done. Still, he looked like she was a meal he couldn't wait to savor.

"No, not now." He reached out and tugged the button open on her pants. Nyah didn't move while he lowered the zipper and pulled the jeans over her hips. When they hit the floor, she stepped out of them and flicked them to the side. Now she stood in just her bikini panties. He ran a curled finger over her mound and paused when he came across her clit. A gentle stroke with the thin material covering her made her quiver and moan. Ethan leaned forward and drew in a deep breath. "Your scent drives me insane. Do you know I can smell it, that you're wet?"

Nyah laid her hands on his shoulders. She let her head go back and lowered her eyelids. When he stuck a finger in the elastic at her thigh and drew it away from her snatch, she gasped. "Ethan."

He grazed her swollen clit with the tip of his tongue. She willed him to continue, but he stilled and rested his forehead on her belly. "I love torturing myself with your body, giving myself a little and then holding off until I am out of my head. Maybe I should let you dance… No, I don't want my hands off you." His hold tightened. "So many men touched you tonight, Nyah."

His words were accusing, yet there was no anger in his tone. She pushed her fingers in his hair. "Just my hand. Only your boy had the nerve to put his hands at my waist. Luke is crazy."

"Stop." She jumped at the word because now he was angry. "I don't want you to say his name when you're like this. When you're turned on and so wet your pussy is dripping with your sweet honey. Forgive me for being jealous."

Was he kidding? It was a turn-on, and he was just possessive enough to make her feel special without being neurotic. A woman had to love that.

"Whatever you want, baby." She'd tested it out, the endearment, and waited for his response.

"Mm," he said. Had he noticed? Ethan didn't appear to want to focus on anything but her pussy, and she didn't mind a bit. He stuck his tongue out again and laved her pussy juices. She was as wet as she was that last time, almost dripping down her thighs. Ethan chased after every drop with his hungry mouth, yet he didn't remove her panties. He wanted to fight for it, make it more difficult. Somehow she thought it was hotter to be partially clothed while having sex.

"Tell me what you want me to do," she whispered.

He reached behind her and pushed fingers beneath her

panties to cup her ass. "I want you to stand here and let me explore your sexy body." And then he seemed to come up with another idea. "Tell me something."

"Yes?"

"Will you be offended if I tear off your panties?"

Her *eep* was about excitement rather than the loss of her undies. "N-No, I wouldn't."

"When I take you back downstairs, I want you to walk among them with no panties and no bra beneath your clothes."

"Okay."

She shivered when he hooked a finger in the front of the panties and tore them apart. How had he done it? Two strips lay in his big palm when he was done. Her heart raced so hard, it was almost painful. Nyah shook from head to toe.

"I'm sorry, honey, are you cold?" He raised her from the floor and deposited her on the bed. She lusted after his contracted biceps as he held her. They strained against the fabric of his jacket, and he made an impatient sound as he straightened above her and whipped it off. Nyah watched his fingers move with lightning speed as he undid each button of his shirt, and then that too was flung aside. Her mouth watered at the sight of his bare chest. She extended hands to touch, but he caught them, kissed her fingertips, and laid her hands down. "You don't do anything. Let me feast on you first."

"I know you want to feel pleasure too," she protested. "Let me please you, baby."

"Not yet." He squeezed the backs of her thighs, massaging them. Somehow being so close to her pussy sent zings of need to her core. He worked his way down toward her knees and then back up, almost to the top where with just a small movement, his thumbs would dip into her cream. Of course, he didn't let that happen, and she chewed her lip.

Ethan stuck his tongue between her folds and laved until she heard the sounds of him licking her come. Nyah cried out and raised her hips. He stopped and pushed her down.

"No, lie still."

"How can I, damn it! That feels good."

He chuckled. "I know, but I don't want you to come too soon."

"I thought this was about torturing you, not me."

He kissed her pussy and grinned at her. "It is, but when I draw it out for you as well, you come much harder. Now tell me you don't like that, Nyah."

"I'd be lying," she murmured. "Eat me some more, Ethan, please."

This time he stuck a thumb in her, and she squirmed. He held her still, working his digit in and out and alternating that with licking her clit and circling it with his thumb. Every time she jerked ready to fall into an orgasm, he pulled back and returned to her thighs. When he wasn't touching her pussy in some way, he blew on it. The cool breeze teased her senses and made goose bumps pop out along her arms.

"Mm, yes, you know how to get me hot, but I can't take

it anymore. You've got to let me come, Ethan."

"Not yet."

She shoved at him and somehow got free to crawl higher on the bed. Ethan chased after her. He caught her ankle, pulled, and she fell flat. He pinned her down with his huge body and raised her hands above her head.

"No more teasing," she demanded.

"Did I not say you belong to me, honey? And you didn't disagree." She heard him working with the front of his pants, and then his rigid cock brushed her ass. Nyah shrieked in frustration and pushed her ass to his crotch. She got a hand loose only to have him grasp it again and force it to the pillow. When he began pumping against her ass, his cock sliding between her legs but not going in, she lost all strength to fight him. His lips touched the sensitive area beneath her ear. "I may take you through a lot to get there, but I will always pleasure you, Nyah. I will never leave you wanting."

"Y-You want me at your mercy," she accused him, hating how her voice shook. The man knew damn well what he was doing, and her stupid body was all of it. She arched her ass higher, and he met it with a thrust but no penetration. She whined, dropping her face to the pillow.

"Just stay there," he said and moved down her body again.

Nyah wasn't one to obey orders. She leaned up a little and peered over her shoulder. When she saw what he was about to do, her eyes widened. "You can't do that!"

"Watch me." He pushed her ass cheeks apart. Nyah

almost chewed her lip off. And then his tongue pierced her. Not at her anus as she first thought, but lower at her pussy. The fact that he did with her laying facedown got to her though, like it was risky or something. Her pussy weeped, cream flowing, and Ethan licked it all.

He alternated between driving his tongue into her and eating the come. A shock of pleasured rocketed through Nyah's core when she came. She struggled to stay where she was because she didn't want him to back off again. He kept licking, and then he had to burrow deeper to get to her clit. Nyah cried out his name. She raised her hips higher. One swipe of her sensitive bud, and she came again. Ethan captured her clit between his lips and sucked hard. She scratched at the pillow and covers, tearing the neatly made bed apart. Ethan didn't let up for a second. He kept coming at her, holding her in place with strong hands she couldn't escape from. His strength and his tongue turned her on like she'd never been before.

"I can't…" she panted, her voice muffled with her head having dropped.

He drew back long enough to ask, "You can't what?" Then he went at her again. Ethan pumped his tongue in and out of her like a cock, and she whined.

"I can't…" She swallowed trying to gather her thoughts. "I can't come again. It's too much."

"No, honey, it can never be enough." He smacked at her cheeks and then rubbed the sting away. He followed that with a kiss and another spanking before returning to her pussy. Nyah moaned through half a dozen orgasms before Ethan deemed it time to give her a break.

She lay there a minute with her eyes closed. What man could give a woman oral sex for so long? And for that matter enjoy it. When Ethan sat up and leaned back on his haunches, he ran a finger around the edges of his mouth and licked away her come. She glared at the self-satisfied expression on his face, but he chuckled.

"You're complaining about me satisfying you?"

"No, I mean…" What could she say? He had made her feel good, and all she had to do was lay there and enjoy it. He was amazing, and what made it worse was that he knew it.

Ethan grabbed her ankle and gave it a gentle squeeze. "I could have gone on a much longer time, but your endurance of multiple orgasms isn't there yet."

She flipped over and sat up. "Hey, I'll have you know I could—"

His eyebrows went up. "Yes?"

She rolled her eyes at him. "Nothing."

When he crawled up the bed on all fours like a feral beast, she scooted backward. He tsked and shook his head then grabbed her at the calf. One quick movement, and he lay on top of her. Nyah ran her hands up his chest while she looked him in the eyes. She knew a challenge lay in hers, wanting him to know she wasn't afraid of his prowess. A lesser woman would be intimidated, but she was beyond all that. At least she wanted him to think so.

She curled her legs around him, running her feet up his strong thighs. She arched and pushed her breasts into his chest. He groaned and dropped his head to suckle at one nipple. A gentle tug on the tip had her lips parted and her eyelids fluttering closed. The thick cock between them twitched to get inside her.

"Put it in, Ethan," she whispered. "You know you want to." The shaft lay against her thigh where he'd guided it because each time it slipped between her legs, the head met with her opening. Something told her he had trouble not letting it bury itself deep into her channel.

"Protection," he said.

She stiffened, and her fingers spasmed on his biceps.

"Don't worry. I have a condom in my pocket," he assured her.

"Just in case you seduce random women in your old bed?" she offered.

He kissed her lips, a long drawn out caress that had her clinging to him. "Not random. Specific. *You.*"

She nuzzled his neck, fighting for control. "Don't say that."

He lifted her chin and kissed her again. She melted into his embrace. *Oh, damn, damn, damn. I love him.*

He drew back from the kiss to look in her face, but she ducked her head and slapped his shoulder. "The condom, man. You're still making me wait."

"Fine."

She heard the smile in his voice but kept her gaze lowered so he wouldn't see the love in her eyes. He sat up and reached over the side of the bed to grab his pants. The packet was torn open, and he rolled the condom on his cock. Nyah lay on her back, legs spread, waiting for him to fill her. He paused when he looked up from his task, to take in the picture she made. Wanton slut, she guessed with amusement.

"Are you aware of just how beautiful you are?" he asked.

She pushed her lips out and went for sarcasm. "Of course." Running a hand over her breasts and then down her belly, she gave him an inviting look. Yeah, hiding her feelings for him behind seduction was easier. Her fingers impacted her clit, and she tweaked it between her first and middle finger. He watched every movement, lust glazing his eyes. Nyah dipped the two fingers into her wetness, and he hissed.

Ethan came forward and pushed her hand away. She didn't have time to do more than draw a breath before his big cock buried itself to the hilt inside of her. He lay atop her and reached down to grip her ass, lifting her slightly off the bed. His thrusts were rough and hard. Nyah couldn't control her cries of ecstasy. She forgot for a moment where they were and let herself enjoy every pump and grind.

Ethan's cock was so thick and amazing, he destroyed her for every other man. She raised her knees and held onto them, taking all he had to offer. Their bodies slapped together over and over. Ethan growled her name and pulled her hair. Her head went back, and he claimed her throat with his lips.

"No, no," he grumbled. "I'm going to come. Too soon!"

He thumped into her harder, and the poor old bed gave evidence of what they did with noisy squeals in the springs. Nyah lost all her strength. She couldn't even hold onto him or gyrate her hips to match his rhythm. He didn't seem to mind. Ethan shifted his weight, and all of a sudden, she felt him at a whole different angle, stimulating her body to the point that she was about to come again.

"Oh my gosh, Ethan, what did you do?" she whimpered. His cock head found her sweet spot, and it was all she could do not to scream her head off. Her core muscles contracted, and the pleasure radiating from her center had her spiraling out of control. Ethan skimmed her back with both hands and stopped at her shoulder blades. He yanked her forward and drove deep.

Nyah fell—hard and loud. She cried out his name and scratched his back. Their bodies writhed together as if they had minds of their own. She heard him somewhere beyond her own cries as he grunted her name. By the jerk of his hips and the tightening in his hold, she knew he came.

When they were done, he lay her flat on the bed and rolled carefully away. Nyah moaned as she tried lowering her legs. Her thighs ached. Ethan reached out and helped push them down, and she moaned again.

"Sorry about that." He grinned and kissed her.

"Liar."

They smiled at each other, and then the pounding on the door started. Nyah froze. Oh hell, what had she been thinking having sex here with Ethan. This was his family home, but still his sister lived there with her family. They'd basically gone to someone else's house and had sex in one of the rooms. Shame and embarrassment washed over her.

"Hey, you two," Luke called through the door. "Having all the fun without me? I wouldn't interrupt, but you know who sent me to put a stop to it."

Nyah slapped a hand between her legs and an arm over her breasts like Luke could see through the door. "Damn it, Ethan. Look what you got me into. Now I have to walk down there in front of everybody, and they'll know what we were doing up here."

He stood up like none of it made any difference to him and reached a hand out to help her up. "It's not a big deal, honey. Every one of those men down there, including my idiot friend Luke, knows what it's like not to be able to wait. Anne wanted me at this party, so…" He shrugged and trailed off.

"And because of that she deserves to have all her guests hear us doing the nasty." She sucked her teeth and shook her head trying not to laugh. "You know you're wrong, right? No shame at all."

"None." He smacked her ass as she bent over to grab her clothes. Nyah bit off a yelp and moved out of his reach. She searched the floor and under the bed for her torn panties and couldn't find them. Ethan was already dressed and waiting when she looked up at him. The innocent expression wasn't fooling anyone.

"Where are my panties, Ethan?"

He didn't even try to pretend he didn't take them, but patted his pants pocket. "Here. They're beyond repair.

Besides, you promised me you'd go downstairs without them."

"I don't remember promising."

His gaze dropped to her bare breasts, and he made no attempt to comment again. She swore and wiggled into her jeans. Of course they weren't that comfortable since she was a mess and needed a shower. Panties would have made it bearable, but she did feel a spark of excitement too. If she knew Ethan at all, he'd want more of her later. Underwear would only get in the way as they worked out of their clothes at her place. But first a shower. She didn't care what he said.

"I should have made you leave yours off too," she quipped.

He strolled to the door and put a hand on the knob with a wink. "I don't wear panties."

She rolled her eyes at him and preceded him out the door. Luke stood leaning against the opposite wall and broke into applause when he spotted them. Nyah directed a raised eyebrow at him and curled her lips, hoping to wither him where he stood. The idiot just grinned back at her. Apparently, he didn't have shame either.

As she drew alongside him, Luke gave a stiff bow. "My beauty, I wish I was the one making you scream like that."

"You've had too much to drink, Luke," Ethan snapped. "Go home."

"Yes, sir, boss," was his friend's quick response, and he followed them down the hall still smiling from ear to ear.

Her embarrassment didn't start easing up until Nyah

came face to face with Mandy at the bottom of the stairs. The rage in the eyes and the pink cheeks was enough to put Nyah's world right again. She sauntered on past the woman, head held high, and continued into the front hall of the house. Something told her Anne wouldn't respond if she said her good-byes to her, so she called a general farewell to those nearest and waved. Just as Ethan had said, every one of the men's eyes whose she met held longing, and many of the women were pissed. Some seemed like they didn't give a damn either way, and of course the couple she suspected were a part of Anne's entourage appeared ready to jump her. *Bring it on*, she challenged without a word. The women's eyes dropped. *That's what I thought.*

Outside cars were pulling out, and valets drove up others for departing guests. She wondered where they were earlier and then figured they'd been in the kitchen or one of the rooms she'd yet to see in the huge house. As soon as Ethan moved behind her, one of the men called out, "I've got it, sir," and rushed off she guessed to pull his car around. The GT500 shined in the moonlight. Ethan edged the valet out of the way to open her door himself and help her inside. Nyah folded in and watched Ethan walk around to the driver side. He got in and turned over the engine but paused when the front door of the house opened. Nyah muttered a "here we go" when she saw Anne hurrying out. Ethan's lips compressed into a straight line. He hit the power button and lowered his window.

"Anne, it's late—"

"I want to know what I've ever done to you that you

would do this to me, Ethan," she demanded. "To bring your whore to my party is…is…" She held a tissue up to her nose, and tears filled her eyes. At that point, Nyah didn't feel a bit sorry.

She leaned forward in her seat pinning Anne with her glare. "I know you did not just call me a whore." She would have said a whole lot more, but Ethan put a hand on her thigh. If he defended the bitch, he was going down with her, but when she looked at him, she realized the seeming quiet calm he displayed wasn't what he was feeling.

"You owe Nyah an apology," he said to Anne in a tight voice.

"What?" she shrieked. "Why should I apologize to her? It was my party, and she ruined it with her common—"

"Three seconds," he interrupted.

Anne fell silent. She peered at Ethan, and whatever she saw in his gaze seemed like it was something she hadn't seen before. Nyah wondered at the way she shivered and tore at the tissue in her hands. She didn't even look at Nyah when she muttered her apology. *Hm, push Ethan's buttons and who's the oldest doesn't matter.*

"Now let me say this," he went on. "I did not mean to disrespect you or your husband in the place you live. But unless you forget this is *my* house. I'm thirty-eight years old, and I listen to your many lectures because you are my older sister, but you will not under any circumstances *ever* disrespect Nyah or any woman I choose to bring around my family. Is that clear?"

Nyah frowned. First, it surprised her that this house was

his and not theirs between him and his sister and brother. Second, she could have felt special since he defended her to his sister and demanded she not get Nyah wrong in that deadly serious tone that might make her think twice if it was turned on her. But he had to ruin the whole affect by adding in Nyah or any other woman. So she was just whoever, and Ethan was pissed more about Anne's attitude in general. She turned her head and stared out the window, schooling her features as if it made her no never mind.

"Yes, that's clear," Anne answered. She straightened and backed away from the car. Ethan threw the car into gear and tore out of the driveway. For a while they rode in silence, and then he reached across to take her hand in his. He drew it to his lips and kissed it. She shivered at the tender caress.

"I'm sorry about that. It was my poor judgment. I shouldn't have seduced you in my old bedroom." The twitch in his lip said he wasn't entirely sorry, and neither was she.

"Please don't even worry about it." She waved her hand. "I like that you defended me, but I'm going to tell you the only reason I didn't knock her down a few pegs was because she's your sister. I've been called a whore and worse, and it does not hurt me. He glanced over at her, and she saw the question. What kind of junk had she gotten in that someone called her a whore? Like she was going to tell him all her past. Rather than answer the curiosity, she pulled her hand from his and laid it on his thigh. A quick sweep had her fingers grazing his cock, and she grinned at his low moan. "So you want to continue this at my place, or what?"

"Without a doubt." His foot slammed on the accelerator, and they sped down the highway.

Chapter Ten

Nyah rode alongside Ethan in his car, taking peeks over at him now and then. They'd been together for a couple months now. He called her when he wanted, and sometimes she told him she was too busy to see him, just to keep a little control for herself. The good thing she could say about the man was that he never just phoned for a bootie call. They went out and did things—the movies, to dinner, bowling, even flying out of town to a mountain resort where he had her trying to ski. That was a trip.

Through it all, he never changed the status of their relationship, considering them just lovers. The more time she spent with him though, the more she loved him. He was funny and attentive. He might have been born with more money than she'd seen in her life, but it hadn't made him snobby like his sister. Thinking about it brought Anne to mind. Since that night at the mansion, Ethan hadn't pushed her to be around his family, and she was relieved. She wouldn't have gone anyway. If she wasn't his girlfriend, then she didn't have to put up with dumb-ass attitudes from small-minded people. Okay, none related anyway. Most people didn't raise an eyebrow at their being together. Interracial dating was commonplace. Every now and then there was one fool, but neither of them gave a damn, so it was all good. The key word with the subject was "nonrelated."

"Are you sure about this?" she asked him for the hundredth time.

He laughed and grabbed her hand. She let him lace his fingers through hers and kiss the back of her hand as was his habit. "I'm sure. It's not a big deal, Nyah."

"No, you don't know how over-the-top my family can be."

She bit her lip thinking about them, especially her father. How would he react? How would Ethan? Her lover still didn't get casual much. He'd worn a collared shirt and slacks to the movies the other day because she'd forgotten to insist he wear a T-shirt. She'd cracked up when she found out he'd had to go buy one the last time.

He reached out and tugged her lip from between her teeth, and she smacked his hand. "You insist on dressing like that." She frowned at him, scanning him from head to toe. Okay, he did look good, and he had given in to not wearing a tie.

"I'm casual." He fiddled with the extra button she'd loosened when they got in the car, and she slapped his hand again. He pinned her with a good-natured glare. "Are you ashamed of me, Nyah?"

"Are you insane? My sisters will want to sop you up with a biscuit even if they are married or only date black guys."

Amusement brightened his sexy eyes. "A biscuit, huh?"

"Yeah." She tapped a finger on the door at her side. "But you didn't have to come just because I asked you. I just don't want you to feel…"

"Nyah, stop second-guessing it. It's not like we are spending Thanksgiving there together." Which meant what? He continued, "We're just having a Saturday afternoon early dinner."

The man had no idea. Her family spent Thanksgiving Day and the next three days together, celebrating, "being thankful," and having a good time. This was their tradition. She hadn't asked him to Thursday night's feast because one, he was spending it with Anne and her family, and two, she didn't want him to tell her no.

"Yeah, it's just dinner," she said, knowing her family would think differently. She shouldn't have risked it, especially with her father.

Ethan squeezed her hand. "Honey, you put up with Anne and Mandy. I think I can deal with anything your family throws at me."

Yeah what about Mandy, she wanted to ask. She was *not* family. Before she could ask him about it, her cell phone rang in her pocket, and she fished it out. The display flashed *Ma*. They had all chipped in and bought her mother a cell phone last Christmas. The fact that she'd learned to use it and stopped being intimidated to the point of hiding it in her drawer impressed Nyah.

"Hey, Ma," she said. "What's going on?"

"Nyah, are y'all almost here? I can't wait to see you and your boyfriend."

"He's not…uh…" Ethan glanced at her with curiosity in his expression. There was no way she was going to say Ethan and she were lovers and friends. "We're about twenty minutes away. Dad back from the shop?"

"Yes, he's here with Junior. Of course you know they're out there in the garage and the living room TV is blaring a football game." Her mother made a sound of annoyance. Nyah couldn't blame her. She hated that, but the men felt it was all a part of the holiday, and her mother never crossed her father. Later, she knew they'd be out in the backyard playing football themselves. They could have at it.

"What kind of mood is he in?" she asked.

Her mother sucked her teeth, something she'd popped Nyah and her sisters on the legs for as being unladylike. Times changed. "He's happy as long as he has his hands dirty and head under a hood, you know that. When have the two of you talked last?"

"Ma, I was there on Thursday, remember?"

"And you hardly spoke a word to each other!"

Nyah sighed. "I'll talk to you when we get there. Love you. 'Bye."

"Everything okay?" Ethan asked when she tucked her phone away.

"Mm," she mumbled, not wanting to discuss it.

With her stomach in knots, they flew down the highway toward *her* family home.

A short while later, they pulled up to the rancher she'd been raised in. A big wheel had been abandoned by one of her nieces since none of her siblings had given birth to boys yet. The front door opened, and her sister came running out yelling, "Sealiieeee."

Nyah cast a glance in Ethan's direction and broke out into a grin. She couldn't help playing along. It was their thing. "Nettieeee," she cried and ran to hug the sister closest to her age, Connie. They rocked back and forth in each other's arms.

"Oh goodness, here y'all go," her youngest brother exclaimed as he left the house behind Connie. "You two just saw each other two days ago."

Connie rolled her eyes at him. "Don't hate, Michael. You just jealous."

Nyah laughed. "I know, right?"

"Mmhmm," Connie said, and then she spotted Ethan. "Oh wow, Nyah done got herself a white man."

"Connie!" Nyah shrieked.

Michael held out his hand. "Hey, don't mind my rude sisters. "I'm Michael, Nyah's youngest brother." Ethan shook his hand and offered his name as well.

"Y'all, come on in the house off the street," Nyah's mother called from the doorway. "The neighbors are already looking out the windows."

They trooped into the house, and while Nyah loved the home she grew up in, she couldn't help comparing it to the mansion Ethan owned. They could afford nice things because her father made good money, but nowhere near the level Ethan and his family were on. The four-bedroom house was cramped with so many people present. Her parents, sisters, and brothers, along with their kids. No one turned down the invite to spend the entire weekend here, even if it meant doubling up in the rooms and putting out pallets on the floor.

Nyah introduced Ethan to everyone present, and he seemed calm enough, even comfortable talking. Not that she thought he'd fumble for words to say. The man was the director in finance at his company, but still there were situations where everyone would be out of their element.

She hadn't seen her father or her older brother come in though. "Ma, did you tell him we're here?" she asked.

Her mother nodded and folded her hands over the apron she seemed always to be wearing ever since Nyah was a little girl. Nyah took a minute to survey her mother. She looked good for her late fifties, even though Nyah saw new wrinkles around her eyes and lips. She wore the requisite dress and what she called sensible shoes. Nyah hadn't missed how Connie and her other two sisters wore dresses when they came over, but she knew for a fact that Connie at the least wore pants all the time at home and work. Her mother was old-fashioned, and no one upset her, or they risked facing her father's wrath.

"I told him. I guess he'll be in, in a minute." Her mother laid a hand on Michael's shoulder. "Michael, you show Ethan where he can hang his and Nyah's jacket. You can help me finish up in the kitchen, Nyah."

Tugging on the miniskirt that Tracy had forced her to buy, Nyah followed her mother. She'd paired the denim skirt with tights to keep her legs warm, but that didn't help her feel any more confident that her ass wasn't hanging out.

For an hour, she helped her mother while chatting with her sisters, all the time wondering how Ethan was getting along with Michael and if her father and oldest brother would bother coming into the house to at least say hi. The back door opened, and she didn't look up upon hearing heavy feet being stomped and scraped over the rug in that area. The scent of his pipe reached her before he spoke, the smell clinging to his clothes.

He strolled over to the sink and ran water. Nyah glanced up. She set down the spoon she'd been using to stir her mother's famous potato salad, and her hand went to her hip before she forced it down. "Hello, Dad. I was wondering if you were going to come in and see us."

His brown eyes narrowed on her. "Are you sassing me, Nyah?"

"No, sir." She kept her head held high but her expression neutral.

He studied her from head to toe. "I saw you couple days ago? Didn't expect you to come back since you refuse to stay the weekend like everyone else."

"I have to work. You know that better than anyone else."

He harrumphed. "If you had a regular job like a woman

should have, you could get the time off."

"Oh come on," she snapped. "When are you going to accept that I'm a mechanic? I'd think you'd be flattered that I followed in your footsteps."

"I didn't need you to follow me, Nyah," he boomed. "You're a lady. You should act like one."

She ground her teeth and balled her fists. This was the same fight they always had. When she opened her mouth to come back at him, her mother cut her off. "This isn't the time to argue. It's a time for thanksgiving. Now, Nyah, where's your boyfriend so Daddy can meet him."

Nyah sighed, but she didn't have to answer as Michael chose that moment to walk into the kitchen along with Ethan. Junior, who'd been quiet, nodded to her lover, but Michael didn't introduce them first. Ethan walked to her side and faced her dad. Nyah's stomach couldn't get any tighter.

"Dad, this is Ethan. Ethan, my dad," she said.

She waited with bated breath for her father's response and breathed easier when the two men shook hands and offered a "nice to meet you."

After that, everything seemed to flow better. They gathered as many around the dining room table as they could and then assigned the kids to living room with paper plates and napkins.

Nyah sat next to Ethan, who had been seated right next to her father, to her surprise. Usually, her mother arranged her table by order of ages, and that spot was reserved for Connie's husband.

In the middle of dinner, Connie leaned over to whisper in her ear. "Dad told Ma to put Ethan next to him. I think he wants to give him the third degree."

Nyah rolled her eyes. Up to that moment, conversation had been general and stuck to current events or sports. She should have known it couldn't last.

"So, Ethan," her father began, taking on a more serious tone than he'd used up till now.

"Dad, you want some more potato salad?" Nyah blurted. "I know it's your favorite."

He cast her a withering glare, and she fell silent. *I'm an adult, damn it. I can tell him to butt out of my business.* But the respect was too deeply ingrained.

Her father looked back at Ethan. "What are your intentions regarding Nyah? She's the only one of my children without kids of her own, and she's not getting any younger. Are you playing house, or is this serious?"

Forks halted midway to mouths, conversation stopped, and Nyah swore under her breath. Her mother glanced her way, but she was sure she hadn't heard what she said. Every head turned toward Ethan to see what he would say. Nyah laid her hand on his thigh under the table. He didn't have to say a word. She'd warned him it might be like this, but still her dad was wrong. She was no young woman of eighteen too innocent to know her own mind.

"Dad, listen—"

"Sir," Ethan interrupted. "With all due respect, what Nyah and I have is between the two of us. I will guarantee you this. I would never do anything to hurt her. I will always take into consideration what pleases her. She is a very special woman, one that I am privileged to know."

While Nyah was feeling all warm and cozy about Ethan's words and his standing up to her dad, her father wasn't so impressed. She caught the anger in his gaze. He wasn't satisfied with Ethan not being specific, but something told her no matter what he said or did, her dad did not intimidate Ethan like a couple of the teenage boys he'd scared off when she was living at home.

Her mother stood. "Okay, gentlemen, you can go into the living room and watch your game. The girls and I will clean this food up, wash the dishes washed, and get dessert."

Ethan, her dad, and the other men stood as well when her mother rose.

"I can help you," Ethan offered.

"Nonsense!" her dad snapped. "Let the women take care of it. You come with us." Her mother shooed him out of the dining room, and Ethan glanced her way at the door. She shrugged and grinned. He followed her dad and the others out of the room.

"Well, that was interesting," Connie said, hooking her arm with Nyah's.

Nyah rolled her eyes. "Interesting is not the word I would have used, and I know Dad is in there harassing him as we speak."

"Girl, please, your man looked like he could handle himself. Let him deal with Dad. The sooner they get the snarling and chest beating over with the better. That way you can spend more time with the family without all the drama."

"When has this family ever lacked drama?" Nyah demanded.

"True."

They dished out cake and pie, already knowing who liked what. Nyah paused with her hand over the german chocolate cake. Ethan didn't like the crunch of the coconut. She slid that one aside and went for the apple pie. This dessert was one of his favorites. The fact that she knew all that told of how much she'd learned about him over the last couple of months, but did it mean they were closer than either of them cared to admit?

Ethan had said she was special and he'd never do anything to hurt her. She wondered if he knew how much it would break her heart when he decided he'd had enough.

"You love him, don't you?" Connie said, and for the second time all conversation ceased. All the women in the kitchen looked at her. If she were lighter, her cheeks would be flaming.

"What? No, it's not like that," she lied.

Her mother put a hand on her hip. "Nyah Jacquelyn Trainor, don't you lie to me!"

Nyah chewed her lip and sighed. "Ma, I was talking to Connie. Anyway, if y'all have to know, Ethan and I are just friends. Nothing else. He's not my boyfriend, okay?"

"Your eyes are saying something different," her mother asserted.

"Well, *they* are lying."

"Uh-huh." Connie sucked her teeth, earning herself a smack on the arm from her mother. "Ma, you do it too."

"Yes, you girls have corrupted me. In my day…"

"Aw, goodness, here we go," several of them said, and Nyah laughed. She breathed a sigh of relief that the conversation steered away from her love life and turned to their mother's philosophy on how to capture and keep a man—by being a lady at all times. Despite herself, Nyah couldn't help wondering if Ethan would prefer that she was more feminine and cutesy. Mandy certainly was, and she didn't think it was her looks that made Ethan keeping the woman at arm's length.

They joined the men in the living room a short while later, and Nyah found a seat near Ethan. She'd noticed that he was talking with her father before she and the other women came in and wondered what that was about. Ethan didn't mention it. He just took her hand and laced his fingers between hers. Nyah resisted the urge to drag him out in the hall and demand to know what he told her dad. Then she took a deep breath. She was no longer a teenage girl, scared of what her father thought. But deep down, she'd always wanted his approval, and that hadn't changed just because she was nearing thirty.

"Football," Junior announced, and her mother frowned.

"It's already blasting in my living room, Junior," she reprimanded him. "We don't need to turn it up louder."

Nyah chuckled. She knew what her brother was talking about even if it took her a moment to catch on. All the guys, having scoffed down their dessert, stood up. Junior narrowed his eyes on Ethan. "You up for a game, pretty boy?"

"Oh wow, really, Junior?" Nyah snapped. "Ethan isn't dressed for…"

Ethan gave her hand another squeeze and stood up. "Sure, why not?"

Amid her protests, the men all filed out of the house into the back yard. A couple of Michael's friends had joined them, along with her brother-in-law, and her brothers, so they had plenty of bodies. Connie came over to Nyah and jerked her to her feet. "Come on. Let's go watch. We'll see if your pretty boy knows how to handle himself on the field."

"Not you too, Connie."

Her sister laughed. "What? You know he's sexy as hell. Junior's probably jealous. Come on. It will be fun."

They threw on their coats and grabbed some blankets for good measure, then took up spots on patio chairs her mother had left out. The men gathered in the center of their big backyard going over who would be on what team. Nyah spotted her father walking toward the garage on the side of the house. A few years ago, he would have joined the guys, but she guessed he was getting older.

Her mother came out of the house and lit the outdoor fire pit. "The others of us are going to the front to watch over the little ones while they play there. If you two get tired of watching the men, join us."

"Okay, thanks, Ma," Nyah said. She hadn't taken her eyes off Ethan. She couldn't believe the man had unbuttoned and rolled up his sleeves. In the chill of the day, his ears were red, but he didn't seem to feel it. Was he really going to play ball with them?

Connie leaned over toward the pit and warmed her hands. "You surprised he got out there?"

"Of course," she responded. "If you knew him like I do, you'd know that getting him out of his slacks and dress shirts is a trip. He'd be more comfortable in a board meeting than...well, I guess out there. At least, I thought so. Then again, he's always been willing to do whatever I wanted to, but I figured he was—"

"Slumming?"

"No!" She glared at her sister.

Connie stood up and went searching around the yard. She came back with a few sticks and handed half to Nyah. They put their feet up and began snapping off pieces of the sticks and tossing them into the fire pit. This was just something they did, kind of a way to relax and pass the time.

"Nyah, I hope if you don't admit it to us, you'll at least admit to yourself. You love him, and I've never seen you this way. I like it."

She ducked her head and stared the red coals. "Yeah, well, I don't. I feel vulnerable, and I'm scared." To her annoyance, tears welled in her eyes. "He could hurt me bad, Connie. Really bad because...."

Her sister waited.

"You're right. I do love him," she whispered so the guys wouldn't hear. Not that they would given how noisy they were. "He's amazing. In all kinds of ways."

"Oh, really." Connie gave a low moan and swept Ethan with a lusty gaze. Nyah slapped her arm.

"Cool it."

Connie laughed. "Don't worry. I can look, but I am devoted to the fool who just fumbled the ball." They both yelled out encouragement to Connie's husband who raised his hands and then bowed in their direction. Connie sucked her teeth. "He has no sense of embarrassment whatsoever."

"None," Nyah agreed.

"So what are you going to do about Ethan?"

She shrugged. "I don't know. Hang in there, I guess. I mean I enjoy every minute with him. He doesn't just come over for booty calls. You know what I mean?" Her sister nodded, and she went on. "It might end. It might go on for a few years. I'm going to stay with it as long as it lasts."

"Nyah."

She jumped at her dad's call and wiped a few stray tears from her cheeks. With a quick glance at Connie, she stood and walked over to where her father stood. He turned and strolled toward the garage. Nyah couldn't believe he was leading her there. Maybe he intended to stop at the door. But instead, he walked across the sacred threshold and waited for her to enter. She hesitated.

"Come in," he said in a flat tone like it was no big deal. She knew it was.

"Dad, I thought I wasn't allowed in here. None of us girls were. Not even Ma to bring you a snack or whatever."

He grunted. "Are you coming in here or not!"

She darted in, and he closed the door. Nyah stood where she was and watched as he bent over the car he'd been restoring little by little for years. He'd done favors for neighbors and friends, and fixed issues with the family's cars in this garage along with his full-time shop, so his special project often took a backseat. Still, that made it more fun, those stolen moments.

"What did you need, Dad?"

He glared at her for her impatience. "I wanted to talk to you about that man you're dating."

She frowned and crossed her arms, shifting her weight from one foot to the other. "His name is Ethan."

Another look, but Nyah stood her ground. He sighed. "Ethan. I don't like that you're seeing him. You should be with your own kind. Not that I'm prejudiced, but you'd have a much easier life and so would your kids."

"This is not the nineteen sixties, Dad. No one bats an eye much."

"It's the south, isn't it?"

She didn't feel like arguing.

He went on. "I have nothing against him. I talked to him a bit. Seems intelligent. Uses his mind more than his hands, and I can respect that." He pointed a tool toward the parking lot. "That car he's driving says he has money, and from our conversation, he's not a complete fool about what's under the hood."

Nyah knew that was the best compliment her dad could give Ethan. "Thanks, Dad. But like he said, it's not serious between us and—"

"Who says it isn't?" he interrupted. He's here, isn't he? No man lets you take him home to your mama if he's not serious about you. Doesn't matter if he's black or white."

"Dad…"

"He loves you, Nyah."

She froze. "D-Did he say that?"

"Didn't have to. I can see it in him, the way he talks about you, the way he looks at you." Her dad scratched his cheek and left a smudge there. "Like I said, I don't prefer him, but you're grown. He's not a bad man. I told him flat out in front of all the other men in our family that we will kill him if he hurts you."

She shrieked. "Dad, you did not say that."

"I did!"

Nyah ran a hand over her face. "Oh, goodness, I'm surprised we're not on the road speeding home already. Why y'all threatening Ethan?"

Her dad waved a wrench. "I did the same with the others, especially Connie's fool of a husband. She loves him. He treats her well. That's all that matters, but I let him know just like I let yours know. No funny stuff. A blunt object will do the trick." He held up the tool, and Nyah thought she was going to faint. This crazy man was dead serious, but she loved him for it.

"Okay, Dad. I'm sure Ethan was good and warned."

He peered at her as if he tried to gauge whether *she* was serious. Then he turned back to his work. "Come over here, Nyah. Help me with this."

She blinked. "Really?"

He didn't say anything, but his frown said he didn't joke about cars. Nyah didn't question the change of heart. She flew to his side and finished out a very interesting day that she'd never forget.

Chapter Eleven

Ethan stood in the doorway to his bathroom watching Nyah sleep on his bed. He'd let her go first in the shower after their long day at her parent's place even though he'd needed the cleanup more. The sheet she'd thrown over herself had slipped low, exposing her breasts. He liked the view, but he wanted to see more, a lot more. While he stood there, he wondered if he should disturb her. Maybe she needed the rest after the stress of visiting family. One thing was for certain, when he was done dealing with Anne, a strong drink came in handy.

Thinking about family, he recalled what he'd overheard toward the end of the visit. The football game had ended because night was falling, and it was getting increasingly hard to see. Maybe because he was the new guy to the group, he'd been saddled with the responsibility of putting the ball away in the shed. No big deal. Ethan had jogged over, dragging an arm across his forehead. His shirt was plastered to his sweat-soaked body, and his muscles were tighter from the constant exercise. Yet, it felt good. He'd had fun, and it wasn't often that he let loose and was just one of the guys doing what they did.

Ethan had tucked the ball into the shed, and hearing voices toward the front of the house, he assumed everyone had headed that way. He strolled toward the tall wooden gate that was ajar at the side of the house and stopped at what he heard.

"Nyah, I'm your mother. I know you better than anyone else, and I know when my daughter is in love."

"Ma," Nyah exclaimed. "Let it go."

Ethan's eyes widened. In Nyah's tone was something he'd never heard before, but he couldn't pinpoint whether it was because she spoke with her mother about their relationship or another reason.

"Don't 'Ma' me, young woman," her mother snapped. "You love Ethan. And I don't want you to think I have a problem with that. I don't. Your father and I aren't those kind of people. We want you to be happy no matter what. Skin color is not an issue. It's what's in the heart that's important."

He wanted to stand there longer and hear Nyah's response, but he wasn't in the habit of eavesdropping. Ethan stepped forward and pulled the gate wider. Nyah's mother and sister spotted him first, and then Nyah spun to face him. He'd walked up close behind her so that he towered, and she had to tilt her head back to look him in the eyes. He saw the question in hers of whether he'd heard the topic of their conversation.

Rather than give her an answer, he dropped his hands on her shoulders and drew her closer. She wiggled in his hold. "Ethan, not here." And then her gaze fell to his shirt, and she sucked in a breath. "Oh my goodness, you're dirty."

He grinned. "That's what happens when you play football."

"But your shirt is ruined. That's so not coming out."

He liked the way she spoke, so sassy and different than what he was used to. The vibrant attitude drew him. He brought his arms around her and crushed her to his chest. "I'll buy another."

Nyah screamed and laughed. "Ew, you're all sweaty. Get off me."

Of course, Ethan held her tighter. Nyah went on shrieking, and he tickled her to make her squirm even more. He let her go just enough for her to try turning and running, but then he caught her and dragged her back to him. The second her ass impacted his thigh, his cock grew hard.

"You perv—" She slapped a hand over her mouth and looked at her mother. He glanced up too and froze. Parents. It had been a while since he'd dealt with them. Ethan thought he should let her go, but if he did, Nyah's mother would see his hard-on and either toss him out on the curb or be embarrassed. He wanted neither of those to happen. Nyah stopped squirming. "We should get going. It's getting late."

He'd agreed, and soon after good-byes were said all

around. On the road home and now watching her, Ethan went over in his mind what Nyah's mother had said. Was it true? Had Nyah fallen in love with him? He'd never meant that to happen, but he had been too single-minded, thinking only of having her as his lover.

He snapped out of the memory of the day when she spoke.

"Hey." Her eyelids were heavy with sleep as she peered at him. When she stretched and moaned, his cock grew erect. This time he had no reason to hide it. Her gaze lowered to take in his naked form. "Are you tired?"

He grinned and started for the bed. "Don't you know me by now?"

* * * *

Nyah watched Ethan walk over to the bed and put a knee up on the side. She reached for him, and he laced his fingers with hers. She loved when he did that. For some reason, it made her feel special, like she was cherished. Back at her parent's house, she had admitted to Connie that she loved him, in so many words, but not to her mother. She wasn't ready to go down that road. And then he'd come out of the back gate just when they were talking about it for the millionth time.

The man's face was like Fort Knox. She wasn't learning anything from his expression he didn't want her to, and it had driven her nuts the whole way home trying to figure out if he'd heard and if he believed what her mother said if he did. But they hadn't discussed it, and Ethan wasn't behaving any differently.

He ran his nose down the length of her neck and breathed deeply. "Mm, you smell good." His lips moved from her throat to her chin and up to claim her mouth. "Good enough to eat."

"Oh no you don't." She pushed at his chest. "You don't let me suck your cock half as much as I want to."

Amusement brightened his eyes, and a brow rose. "Do you crave it?"

"You know I do."

"Then far be it for me to deny my mistress."

Nyah went still. He stroked her cheek. "Nyah? What's wrong?"

With effort, she shook herself. Not once in all this time had he called her his mistress. Why now? After he might have heard what they were saying at her parents' house? Was he trying to put her in her place and make sure she stayed there? Hurt tightened her chest, and she felt tears threaten. She forced a smile and wiggled around him until she was off the bed.

"Nothing. I just need to pee." She started for the bathroom, but he caught her hand and drew her back.

"What's wrong? I can always tell when you're upset."

She rolled her eyes. "Please, you don't know me that well."

"And now you have an attitude." She heard a bite in his tone too. "What have I said to piss you off?"

"I said nothing. Now let it go!"

She tried to jerk away, but he pulled in the opposite direction, just hard enough for her to tumble onto the bed, lined with his length. Lifting up wasn't even possible with him spreading her arms out so that her breasts were flattened against his chest.

"Ethan," she said in warning.

"What?"

She swore. "Let me up. I said I have to pee."

"And I don't believe you." He brought a knee up between her legs and then pushed outward so that her thighs parted. Pissed, she tried not to feel his cock tip pressing against her folds. Desire snaked along her body, whether she liked it or not. *Oh, I like it. Nyah don't even trip.*

"Now I'm not allowed to go to the bathroom?" she said. "You think I'm lying about something that stupid. We had a fun day. Don't ruin it."

He frowned at her, and if anything, his grip on her wrists tightened. He moved them so her hands were flat on his chest. His skin was warm and damp from the shower. The scent of soap clung to it with a mixture of his natural masculine aroma. This was how she liked him to smell and what melted her in his arms. She was a strong woman. She knew that. But she got off on him being more powerful and taking control of her and their activities in bed.

Ethan must have sensed her increased need. She had lowered her gaze from his face to his chin, so he wouldn't see the hurt. He used a thumb to massage the inside of her wrist, and the sensation zinged along her veins, traveling straight down to her pussy. Before him, she would never have guessed a connection like that existed.

He laved her earlobe with his tongue then pulled it between his lips. She shivered, angry and not wanting to give in. Ethan's hot breath there and then farther at that sensitive spot did not help her keep her head.

"I want to fuck you," he whispered, and she could have sobbed. Somehow she knew this wasn't one of his times of talking dirty to her. He'd deliberately avoided the terms "making love."

When she didn't move but was panting—not from excitement but with an effort not to cry, he must have assumed he had calmed her, and he let her wrists go. Nyah sat up on his lap and smiled. The lust in Ethan's eyes alienated her for the first time. She waited another few seconds and then slipped off of him to snatch her shoes and clothes from the floor in one fell swoop.

"I'm not feeling well. I'm going home."

He sat up. "What do you mean you're going home?" When she made no comment, "Nyah!"

"What do you want from me, Ethan? A kidney? Sorry, I can't give you everything."

He threw his legs over the edge of the bed. "Is that what this is about? You're upset about what your mother said? I—"

"Don't you do it," she shouted, pointing a finger at him. "Don't even go there. We're not discussing it."

"We need to be mature about this."

"Mature?" she shrieked. "You did not just accuse me of not being mature. I guess you forgot I'm your mistress now. You want to fuck me!"

Ethan's handsome face clouded like he had no clue what she was talking about. He was not going to play dumb with her. He wanted to talk about it. Oh yeah, they could talk about it, and then she was getting the hell out of here and never coming back.

"Nyah…"

"I'm doing the talking here." She would have continued, but his phone rang. "Who could that be this time of night?" The clock at the side of the bed read just past midnight.

Ethan read the ID on his phone, and his brows crashed low over his eyes. "My niece." He answered. "Kate, what are you doing calling this late? Shouldn't you be in bed… whoa, calm down. I can't understand you."

Fear clutched at Nyah's chest. While he listened to his niece, she pulled on her clothes and looked for something clean for him to wear. Even if this wasn't a family emergency, he'd need to take her home. When Ethan disconnected the call, he looked up at her, and she saw pain and fear flash in his eyes before his face went blank. She hurried over dropped to her knees in front of him. "What's wrong, Ethan? Is it Anne?"

He nodded. "She's been rushed to the hospital in severe pain. Her husband is out of the country. I need to go there."

"Of course. I have something you can put on here." She stood up. "I'll wait until you get back, or if you're out all night, I can take the bus. Don't worry about it. Just go be with your family."

She tried moving out of his way, but he caught her fingers and held on. "If you don't mind…Nyah, I want you to go to the hospital with me."

Her eyes widened. "Are you sure? Anne doesn't like me…"

"I want you there."

"Okay, of course. I'll go. Hurry up and get dressed."

They arrived at the hospital a short time later, and Nyah didn't know what Ethan said to the nurse, but she ended up in the back along with him where Anne had been put in a bed. His nieces, the oldest being sixteen came hurtling toward him and pressed their faces into his stomach. He hugged them tight and knelt down to the one who must have called him. The teenager's face was pale, and she hadn't said a word. So it had been the middle child who thought to call Ethan.

"Wait for me a minute while I go in to see how your mom is doing and what the doctor says, okay?" Ethan told them.

He had trouble dislodging their clinging hands, and Nyah stepped forward. "Hey, y'all must be hungry, huh? How about I buy you a snack from the machines out in the waiting area?"

That got them moving, and Ethan tossed her a grateful look. While she led them out and searched her wallet for money, she wondered where Anne's girlfriends were, someone who could have taken charge of her daughters while she was ill. Was their brother still out of the country too? She didn't get people like them. If anyone in her family was sick, the whole troop would have been there even if it was three in the morning.

The girls had scarfed down chips, candy bars, and soda and were sleeping by the time Ethan reappeared. He walked over and kissed her lips briefly before taking a seat next to her. The worry in his eyes this time didn't vanish, which said the situation might be serious. She waited in silence for him to share if he chose to.

Ethan ran a hand through his hair and glanced at his nieces then back at Nyah. "She had a ruptured cyst on her ovary. That's what caused the pain. Now, they have to do a biopsy to discover if it was cancerous. The doctor gave Anne meds to dull the pain, but she's crying and won't stop. I can't get her to calm down. We've always been pretty healthy." He stood up and began to pace. "I don't know where the hell her friends are at a time like this. No, damn it, I should be able to help her."

He seemed about to go back in, but Nyah jumped to her feet and stopped him. She didn't like seeing him this way. He was always calm and controlled no matter the situation, and she saw the truth in what he'd said, that they weren't used to this. The woman had had three daughters. One would think she was used to pain. But possible cancer was a whole other ballgame, especially with the thought of not being there for her young kids.

"Let me go in," she volunteered. "I have been through this—with my mother. I know how scary it is. We might not be the best of friends, but I think I can help."

"Ethan!"

They both looked around to see Mandy running toward them. Nyah narrowed her eyes. The woman wore a trench coat that flapped open as she moved, revealing a filmy nightgown under it. *Really? She came to the hospital like that?* Nyah tried to give the woman the benefit of the doubt. Plenty of people slept in skimpy night wear, and Mandy must have thrown the first thing she could get her hands on when she got the call.

"Mandy," Ethan said, "thanks for coming." She flew into his arms, and he hugged her. When he drew back, Mandy held on.

"What did the doctor say?" she asked, face upturned to his.

Ethan explained, and blood drained from Mandy's face. She looked like she was about to faint, and Ethan led her to a chair. Nyah sighed.

"I'm going in. I'll be back."

She left them there and walked through the door leading to the back as someone came out. No one stopped her as she made her way to the room where she'd seen Ethan disappear behind a curtain earlier. A she drew closer, she heard Anne's muffled sobs. Nyah paused outside a second and took a deep breath. She ducked behind the curtain.

"Hey, Anne."

Ethan's sister looked up. Her face was tear-stained and blotchy. Her eyes were swollen, and she lay on her back, hooked to monitors. If she was this upset, why hadn't someone knocked her out with more drugs? But then she saw the terror in the woman's gaze, and when the smartass remark didn't come about what she was doing there, Nyah felt sorry for her.

She walked around the edge of the bed and sat down. "So," she began, searching for something to snap Anne out of her pity party, "a strong woman like you shouldn't be blowing snot bubbles with her little girls out there scared silly."

Anne gasped, and then she frowned. "Who the hell—"

"That's better," Nyah interrupted. "Listen, I know you're scared, and we're not exactly the best of friends, but I figured you needed a levelheaded person to help you calm down."

Anne gripped the thin sheet covering her and compressed her lips into a straight line. She stared at the ceiling. "Why are *you* here?"

"Even better," Nyah commented. "You're not crying anymore. See? I did my job. And to answer your question, I'm here because your family and friend…" She rolled her eyes thinking about Mandy. "…are acting like idiots when no one knows if there's anything to be scared about yet."

"Thanks for caring," Anne spat. A tear rolled down her cheek, and despite her obvious desire to get Nyah out of the room, Nyah reached for one of her hands and held it. She leaned in closer and brushed Anne's hair from her face.

"I've been through this. With my mother." She'd pitched her voice lower, and Anne went still at her words. "She too had a cyst on her ovary, about a year ago and a half ago. It was terrifying for all of us, especially my mom and dad, but it's going to be okay. The doctor's going to find the cyst was benign, and you'll be out of here in time for morning tee off at your country club."

Nyah chuckled at that last remark, and for the first time since she walked in, Anne gave a weak smile. She seemed to force her hands flat on the sheet, and she smoothed it out not looking at Nyah. "None of my friends came. Not one. The woman I thought was my closest friend had the gall to tell me she'd just taken a lover, and this was their first weekend away together. She told me to call her and give her an update. Call *her*!"

Nyah sucked her teeth. "Bitches every one of them. Don't even worry about it. They probably were hanging on because you had your stuff together, and they wanted to seem like they were in the know."

Anne blinked, and Nyah laughed again.

"You hate me, but I'm a person, right? Willing to be here." When Anne tried grabbing for a cup of water on the side table, Nyah stood up and retrieved it. "Let me help you with that."

After Anne had drunk some and muttered her thanks, she said, "I don't hate you."

"Well you don't like me, and that's okay too." She shrugged. "I'm sure in a few hours your husband will be here and—"

"No, he won't."

Nyah didn't know what to say to that. The vehemence in Anne's tone was a far cry from her previous sobbing, but it was good to see fire in her eyes if nothing else.

"I didn't call him," Anne admitted. "I guess you heard he's out of the country, but I suspect he's with someone. Ethan never did like my husband, but he had good reason. I caught him cheating I don't know how many times. And it's become abundantly clear that he married me for my money."

Okay, and now we are getting personal. Nyah racked her brain for something to say in response. "I'm sorry."

Anne was on a roll and seemed not to have heard. "That's why I'm so protective of Ethan. I want him to find someone who loves him for himself and not just for what he can offer." She peered at Nyah, and the assessment was almost tangible. "I'm not saying you're after his money, but I don't think you're right for him either. I love my brother, and I don't want him hurt like I am…was."

"That's not for you to decide, though, is it?" Nyah tried hard to remember that the woman in front of her was ill and needed support. She hesitated. "Anyway, you don't have to worry about it. Ethan and I are breaking up. I'm not going to see him after today."

She hadn't really thought about it fully, but saying the words helped her realize that's what she'd decided. Ethan didn't feel like she did, and delaying the inevitable was too much, especially now that she knew he'd heard her and her mother talking. Better to shore up her heart now rather than later.

"You're what?" Anne's mouth dropped open. "The two of you just decided that? Or…" She schooled her features. "I mean I hope you'll find the right person for you, and I appreciate you coming here today. Please ask my brother to come back in. I won't freak him out with more tears."

Nyah nodded and stood up. She walked to the curtain and paused to glance back. "What I said about us breaking up. Please don't say anything to him about it."

Anne's eyebrows rose. "Okay."

Feeling satisfied with that, Nyah left the little sectioned off room and headed down the hall and through the door to the waiting area. Ethan spotted her as soon as she came out and surged to his feet. "She okay?"

He put his hands up as if he was about to hug her, but she held him off. "Yes, she's a lot calmer now. She wants to see you."

"Thanks." His smile was so warm, it shook her, and when he lowered his head to touch his forehead to hers, she almost forgot her resolve. Ethan pressed a kiss to her lips and left to go see his sister. Nyah glanced over to where the kids and Mandy sat. All of them were asleep, and Nyah sighed. Mandy was one of them, even if she was just a secretary. Ethan, or maybe Anne, had called her. Mandy fit in.

Ethan had never given her any worries about wanting Mandy or cheating with her while he was with Nyah, but maybe he was overlooking her too. Maybe she was the right one for him. He'd said Mandy was a childhood friend. Once Nyah was out of the way, he could take the woman's feelings for him more seriously. All Nyah wanted was for him to be happy—because it was for sure, she wouldn't be. Not for a long, long time.

Chapter Twelve

"So what are you going to do, Nyah, stay home and hide out forever?" Tracy asked.

Nyah stared at the TV playing a soap opera she wasn't watching. She'd dressed in sweat shorts and a tank top and hadn't showered in like two days. As much as she disgusted her, she couldn't force her butt off the couch. When she told Ethan she was done—by way of phone and not face-to-face because that would have been too much—he'd rushed over to her place to talk it out. She didn't answer the door. And when he decided to bombard her workplace with flowers, she took leave. He knew she didn't like flowers, but it was his way of pushing her into talking to him. She was stubborn and didn't give in. Why wouldn't he give up? After all he could get any stupid ass mistress he wanted!

"Yeah, that's my plan," she sniped. "I'm digging in for the long, hard winter."

"Hate to break it to you, but winters here in Charlotte can hardly be termed 'long and hard.'"

Nyah rolled her eyes. "Whatever. He just wants me to call him and cuss him out for harassment. That would be his way of getting me to talk."

"So why won't you?" Tracy reasoned. "I know you're missing him, and I hear the tears. You're not fooling anyone."

Frustrated, Nyah reached for the remote and clicked the set off. The apartment went from low noise to silence, the perfect atmosphere to make her dwell on Ethan—his eyes, his hands, his body, even his voice. She pressed the heel of her hand against her forehead and slumped back on the couch.

"I'm just waiting," she said. "As time goes on, I'll feel less and less hurt. Then I'll get back on my feet. I was thinking this might be the perfect opportunity to start looking around for my shop. Get it off the ground and throw myself into work. Will you come work for me when I'm up and running?"

"Girl, you know I will." Then Tracy started laughing.

Nyah frowned. "What?"

"Can I call you Nyah the Wonder Boss?"

"Hell, no!"

But the comment did make her laugh, which she hadn't felt like doing since that visit to the hospital to see Anne. Ethan had texted her to let her know his sister was fine. The results of her biopsy showed the cyst had been benign, just like Nyah suspected. She'd texted to tell Anne she was glad. Ethan tried continuing the conversation, but she had switched her phone off and gone to bed.

Remembering that exchange made her wish more than anything that she could talk to him. No, she had to be strong and move on with her life. "I'm thinking about going to stay with my parents for a couple of days. I feel like I might run into Ethan before he gives up."

"Have you considered you might have hurt him by dumping him like that?" Tracy asked.

"Hurt him?" She'd never thought of that. But no, Ethan kept calling because he hated losing. He wanted to be the one to dump her when he was done. Wasn't that how all men were, especially the player types? Yet, while she'd thought his penthouse was something only playboys kept uptown for the women they picked up in the clubs, Ethan had never behaved that way. She hated to think this whole time she'd stereotyped him and hadn't given him a real chance. He never kept to the unspoken rules of men who wanted sex and nothing else. He'd *dated* her.

She had been the one to insist on a date in the first place. He had asked should they go to his place or hers. In the beginning, Ethan had wanted no strings, but that didn't mean it had changed. Had it? His reaction to hearing her mother say she loved him had seemed to take them right back to the start of their relationship. She chewed her lip, going over every detail of what he said and did and came to no definite conclusion.

"You do what you gotta do, girl. And call me, K?"

"Yeah, thanks, Tracy. I'll talk to you later. I'm going to

get moving."

After they said good-bye, Nyah dragged herself off the couch and took a shower. She threw on fresh clothes and packed an overnight bag. She decided not to call her parents to tell them she was coming. They wouldn't turn her away, but she still didn't feel like talking much.

When she was ready, she made sure everything was turned off and grabbed her keys. Safe on the road, she breathed a sigh of relief and settled in for the two-hour drive across the state. A half hour into the trip, blue lights flashed behind her car, and the policeman's siren did that two short burst thing that cops liked to do.

Nyah looked up into her rearview mirror. "Aw, damn," she muttered.

The cop took his time walking up to her window once she'd pulled over. She wondered if it was a brake light out or something. She knew she wasn't speeding because that would take energy, which she didn't have. Her mind felt dulled, so maybe she'd swerved or broken some other law.

"Is there a problem, officer?" she asked when he drew alongside the car.

"License and registration," he said. She handed them over, and he peered at the information above his sunglasses.

When he returned to his car with her license, her stomach cramped, and all kinds of thoughts raced through her mind. What if there was a warrant out for her arrest? What if this was a case of mistaken identity? *Okay, calm down, Nyah. Getting worked up is not going to solve this.*

Through her rearview mirror, she spotted him talking

in the receiver of his CB. A few minutes later, he came back. "Ma'am, I'm going to need you to follow me to this next exit."

"What am I being charged with?" Good. Her voice hadn't shook. That said nothing about the turmoil inside.

"Nothing, yet," he responded, which didn't make her feel better. She nodded in agreement, and followed him. Soon they were on a side road, and the policeman turned into a fast food restaurant's parking lot. Nyah pulled up beside him. Rather than risk making him angry by getting out, she cut the engine and waited. Minutes went by, and she gripped the steering wheel. The cop sat unmoving in his vehicle. Once in a while, he glanced around toward the street where they'd driven in. Was he waiting for someone? *Backup?* Nyah's teeth chattered. Maybe she should call her dad.

Before she could do anything, another car pulled off the street and headed straight toward them. *Impossible. Totally, impossible*, she raged silently when she recognized the Shelby GT500. Sure enough, Ethan unfolded from his car, and the cop got out of his. They spoke a few words with each other and shook hands. Ethan clapped the policeman on the shoulder and headed toward her. He tapped on her closed window, and she ignored him.

"Open the window, Nyah," he said.

She rolled her eyes at him.

"Do you want me to have my cousin arrest you?"

She shrieked and hit the power switch to open the window. "Your cousin! You mean you set this up? Do you know how scared I was that I was in trouble?"

"You *are* in trouble." She flinched when he brought his hands down heavy on her door and bent so they were eye to eye. "You've been avoiding me, and that stops today."

Nyah refused to be intimidated now that she knew what was going on. "Don't you know how to give up when a woman dumps you?"

"You're not dumping me."

She sucked her teeth. "Excuse me?"

Ethan nodded to his cousin, and the man took off. He reached inside her window to unlock her door before she could stop him and wrenched it open. Nyah found herself wedged against his chest with one steel band of an arm around her. Between his hard body and the car, she wasn't going anywhere until he chose to let her go.

"You've been running from me, but that's going to stop, and we're going to talk. Now, you can get in your car and follow me to my place, or you can try to get away again, and I can make a call."

"Meaning your cousin." He released her and stepped back. Nyah folded her arms over her chest, glaring at him. "Let me guess. You're going to have him and his buddies chase me all over North Carolina."

Ethan grinned, so confident, she wanted to smack his handsome face and almost did, but his expression told her he knew he'd pushed her buttons, and he was prepared to push a lot harder.

"I don't think that will be necessary. Do you?" he asked.

"Fine. Whatever." She turned to get into her car. "We can get this over with once and for all."

A short time later, she moved ahead of him into his apartment while he held the door for her. Nyah paused in the middle of the living room, lips tight, attitude rolling off her in waves. She narrowed her eyes at him waiting for his next words.

"I'm sorry," he said.

Her eyes bugged. "Come again?"

Ethan crossed from the door and pulled her arms apart, which she'd folded over her chest. He grasped her fingers, and she thought he was going to kiss them as he'd done time and again while they were together, but he behaved himself. Not that he didn't want her. The desire was there in his intense gaze. She sensed it in the heat of his body when he stood so close. The feelings reflected her own as if it had been years since they last saw each other.

Ethan released one hand to run a thumb over her cheek. "I've missed you, Nyah, and I wanted to say I'm sorry. I screwed up."

Her confusion hadn't lessened one bit. "How so?"

"One, I let you go." He moved closer. She couldn't breathe. He stared at her parted lips. "I let finding out you love me make me act like a young boy with no experience. I'm man enough to admit it scared me. Because…"

Nyah pulled from his touch and blinked hard to keep from crying. "Because you were all about the sex. That's how you are, and it's not your fault. I knew what we were doing from the start."

He turned her head back to face him. "Yes, you knew at the start, but you didn't know that with each moment I spent with you, I fell deeper in love."

Totally didn't see that coming. "Huh? You...fell...in love...?"

Ethan cupped her face with both hands. "Yes, in love. I love you, Nyah. I didn't expect it to happen, but it did, and it threw me. The words kept running through my mind all this time, but I didn't want to face them and what they meant to us. I was happy with the way things were. That way, we were content." He offered a wry smile. "Or maybe it was just me content. You must have been hurt when I started talking like an idiot that night."

She shifted her stance and moved out of his hold. Her back was to him, but Ethan didn't let her get far. He moved up behind her, and she shook just feeling his body lined with hers. "You remember that, huh?" she murmured.

"Yeah, I do." He hugged her tight to him. Her heart pounded in her chest, and she couldn't help pressing her forehead to his cheek. Ethan nuzzled lower to find her lips, and this time he kissed her. She welcomed the caress, featherlight and everything she'd been aching for. He kept his mouth to hers, and she longed to taste his tongue, but he spoke instead. "I juggle millions on a regular basis. Comes with the job. But you—a sexy little mechanic with a sassy mouth—brought me to a place that was new."

She gasped. "You've never been in love?"

"And I never will again." He gave her a little of his tongue, and she sagged in his arms. Ethan lifted her and carried her to the couch to deposit on his lap. "Not with anyone but you. Not ever again."

"You don't know that." She frowned at him. "Nothing lasts forever."

He touched a fingertip to her lips. "You're still trying to protect your heart. I'm telling you I'm never letting you go." His brows dropped low over his eyes, and she shivered at the seriousness that she saw there. "If you run, I will come after you. As long as I know you love me, Nyah, I will find you and bring you back."

"Your love is so intense. I don't know if I can handle it."

He drew her closer. "I'll give you some time, and a little space."

He held up his thumb and forefinger, indicating the amount of space she would get, and she laughed. "That much, huh?"

"It's plenty."

They chuckled together, and Nyah leaned against his chest. She luxuriated in his hold, but her pussy clenched with his hands so close to that spot. Because she hadn't trusted him enough to talk, they'd both been denied, and from the feel of his hard-on under her, she knew he wanted it as much as she did. However, there were a couple items that needed to be said. She drew a deep breath.

"I was wrong, Ethan." She licked her lips. "I'm sorry. I was so scared from day one that you would hurt me, that I didn't give you the benefit of the doubt. I stereotyped you. Even though I wanted you like I've never wanted another man, I didn't believe you could want me back more. I didn't think you'd fall in love, so I was always shoring up my heart, always trying to look down the line to when I'd have to run. At first, I thought I'd accepted our relationship as it was, but now I see I never did. I just pushed the worries to the back of my mind. They were still there, festering.

"To be honest, I don't know how I could have done it differently because I couldn't talk to you about my feelings before you were ready to accept yours. In the end, I didn't have to push you away. We were at the point where I should have been honest, and you even tried to get me to talk. Thank you for that. I love you, Ethan. With all my heart, and if you're willing, I want to try again. I'll accept you for what and who you are."

"And I accept you. Wholly," he echoed. "There's no question of trying again. As far as I'm concerned you were, and are, always mine."

Nyah threw her arms around his neck, happiness soaring inside of her. "Well, if I belong to you, then you are responsible for me."

He quirked an eyebrow. "Meaning?"

"Meaning I'm horny as hell."

His eyes blazed brighter. "Then by all means, my love, let me do my job."

He pinched the button on her jeans open and lowered the zipper. Nyah gasped. "Aren't we going to the bedroom?"

"I'm getting inside your panties right here and now."

She couldn't get wetter with those words. Ethan popped her onto her feet and dragged her pants down with her panties. Nyah stepped out of her shoes and wiggled free of her pants and panties. She kicked them away and stood in front of him in just a T-shirt. The shrunken old thing didn't extend past her ass, but Ethan seemed to like that. He gave her rear a swat and opened his own pants. She peered around his hand and moaned as she reached for his cock. "You're already hard."

"And you're surprised?"

"Not really." She gave his length a long stroke, but Ethan brushed her hand away.

He lifted her at the waist and brought her down on his lap facing him. Nyah didn't resist. She knew he was hot to get into her, just as she was with him. A few days might as well have been a year. Of course, they hadn't had sex every day since they'd started going out, but feeling like they never would again had taken a toll and upped the craving.

Nyah rested her hands on his shoulders and watched as Ethan dug out a condom from his pocket. "You always seem to have one."

"I always want you, so I'm always ready."

"Makes sense." Her pussy clenched as he rolled the covering down his cock. She bit her bottom lip. He was so big and long, sitting like this, they would have to be careful, and Ethan would be forced to take her slowly. Somehow that wasn't a bad prospect. They could prolong it and get lost in the sensation of being joined as one.

Ethan lifted her up just high enough for him to work his cock between her folds. Nyah helped him, using two fingers to part her pussy, which was already juicy with her desire. She sank down in degrees, Ethan controlling how fast with his amazing strength. She ducked her head and leaned into his chest. Gently, they began moving together, slow and easy. Their moans echoed as one, and Ethan murmured words of love against her lips.

Nyah's heart was fit to burst. She couldn't believe this man loved her. He was everything she could ever want and more, and he was hooked on *her*.

Ethan raised her chin to kiss her lips. She shut her eyes, enjoying every feather touch and how full he made her feel. She gasped his name, blinking because the emotions along with the physical pleasure swelled to overflowing. Her lover grasped her hips, raised her all the way up so that his cock head alone pierced her opening, and then he brought her down. He angled his hips, and the tip brushed that sweet spot inside. She keened.

"You're going to make me come," she accused him.

He chuckled at her throat and licked it. "That's the idea."

They moved as one, Nyah clutching his shoulders while she pressed her mouth to his neck. "There it is," she cried. Her orgasm shattered control and had her shaking. Ethan crushed her closer. One hand lay over her ass, and he squeezed, driving himself a little deeper. He kept up his slow pump all the way through her climax until her body began to calm, but just when it did, the hand he held at the back of her head spasmed. She knew he was ready. Ethan went still. He held himself deep inside her heat.

"Nyah."

The harsh whisper shocked her. With pleasure and satisfaction lay also hurt. She let him finish, emptying himself in the condom and then drew away to look into his eyes. What she saw there threw her for a loop. The full impact of her walking away from him hit her like a boulder. She'd wounded him, more than she could have thought possible. The knowledge broke her heart, but it was encouraging too. Nothing made it clearer just how much Ethan loved her.

He eased her off his cock and removed the spent condom before hugging her to his chest. "So we're okay, right?" She smiled at the sternness in his tone.

"Yeah, we're more than okay. We're perfect."

He kissed her until she was breathless and horny all over again.

* * * *

For the second time since he'd known Nyah, Ethan found himself eavesdropping. He hadn't intended to do it, but when he heard her voice outside his office door, he'd been eager to see her beautiful face. She'd been so busy with her new shop that he hardly got to see the woman who owned his heart. He'd rushed around his desk and hurried toward the door. He paused just inside with the door partially open to collect himself. While he had no problem demonstrating to Nyah what she meant to him, he didn't relish the entire office seeing him behaving like a puppy in love. He'd never hear the end of it, especially from Luke. That's when he'd caught the conversation between Nyah and Mandy.

"Ethan's schedule is booked solid," Mandy was saying. "There's no way I can squeeze you in. In fact he and I are supposed to be going to lunch in—"

"Look, bitch," Nyah interrupted. Ethan would have gone out there if Nyah hadn't sounded in complete control. "You need to stop playing games with me. Ethan and I are together. You don't like it? I don't give a fuck. But let me make this crystal clear—keep getting in my way, or for that matter, flirting with my man, and I will grab you by your hair and wipe the floor with you. Now you can take the warning, or you can take the risk. Your choice."

Mandy sputtered, not making any sense. Ethan shook himself and forced the grin off his face then opened the door wider. He stepped out. His heart swelled at seeing Nyah. She'd cleaned up and wore a dress. When had she bought one? Either way he knew it was especially for him, and the material clung to her slender figure, giving him ideas of tearing it off and getting his hands on her soft mocha skin.

"Hello, honey, this is a pleasant surprise," he said, impressed with the cool exterior he presented. He kissed her cheek when he wanted to devour her glossed lips. "Stay here for just a second?"

She nodded, and he went back to his doorway. "Mandy, inside," he ordered.

His secretary flushed, but she obeyed. Ethan made sure not to close the door, and they stopped just inside of his office. Mandy stood in front of him with upturned face and parted lips. Even knowing he wasn't pleased, she tried using her charms on him. He'd always ignored it because it didn't bother him over much. He'd made plain that he had no feelings for her. Now, she annoyed Nyah, and that wouldn't be allowed. Ever.

"We've known each other a long time. You're like family. You always will be. However, you need to understand I am with Nyah. I love *her*, and since you cannot seem to respect that, I'm having you transferred."

Mandy shrieked, and her eyes widened. "What do you mean?"

"Just what I said. I've already spoken with Human Resources. You will be supporting the senior manager in shipping."

"Shipping," she yelled, until he gave her glare that calmed her. "Ethan, that's not fair. I hate shipping. They're all boring."

"You'll have plenty of time to take it up with your new boss." He moved past her heading toward the door. "Now, if you'll excuse me, I'm having lunch with Nyah."

When he exited his office, Nyah tumbled into his arms. The grin on her lips must have mirrored his earlier one. "I knew you were perfect," she said.

"Yes, I am," he teased, and she socked his arm.

He embraced her, drawing her to his side as they walked. "Come on. I hope you have the rest of the day free, because I'm starving." He eyed the front of her dress, liking the low cut. Food might be on the menu, but not until he'd had a long taste of this sweet and sassy woman.

Nyah's big brown eyes twinkled with amusement. "I'm all yours."

Ethan nodded. "Yes, you are."

About the Author

Tressie Lockwood has always loved books, and she enjoys writing about heroines who are overcoming the trials of life. She writes straight from her heart, reaching out to those who find it hard to be completely themselves no matter what anyone else thinks. She hopes her readers enjoy her short stories. Visit Tressie on the web at www.tressielockwood.blogspot.com.

www.ingramcontent.com/pod-product-compliance
Lightning Source LLC
Chambersburg PA
CBHW020125180626
46810CB00004B/1409